# VIRAGO
## MODERN CLASSICS
580

*Rumer Godden*

Rumer Godden (1907–98) was the acclaimed author of over sixty works of fiction and non-fiction for adults and children. Born in England, she and her siblings grew up in Narayanganj, India, and she later spent many years living in Calcutta and Kashmir. In 1949 she returned permanently to Britain, and spent the last twenty years of her life in Scotland. Several of her novels were made into films, including *Black Narcissus* in an Academy Award-winning adaption by Powell and Pressburger, *The Greengage Summer*, *The Battle of the Villa Fiorita* and *The River*, which was filmed by Jean Renoir. She was appointed OBE in 1993.

# LISTEN TO THE NIGHTINGALE

## Rumer Godden

virago

VIRAGO

This paperback edition published in 2013 by Virago Press
First published in Great Britain in 1992 by Pan Macmillan Children's Books
a division of Pan Macmillan Limited

Copyright © The Rumer Godden Literary Trust 1992

The moral right of the author has been asserted

A CIP catalogue record for this book
is available from the British Library.

ISBN 978-1-84408-850-8

Typeset in Goudy by M Rules
Printed and bound in Great Britain by
Clays Ltd, St Ives plc

Papers used by Virago are from well-managed forests
and other responsible sources.

 MIX
Paper from
responsible sources
FSC        FSC® C104740
www.fsc.org

Virago Press
An imprint of
Little, Brown Book Group
100 Victoria Embankment
London EC4Y ODY

An Hachette UK Company
www.hachette.co.uk

www.virago.co.uk

*For Marni (Lady Hodgkin)*
*with grateful thanks*

My grateful thanks to: Miss Pauline Wadsworth MRAD, former dancer with the Royal Ballet Company, teacher and senior ballet mistress at the Royal Ballet School, White Lodge, for her help in matters of ballet; Mrs Sheila Anderson, for her continual and excellent typing and retyping of the book; and Mrs Peggy McKeever, for her patience and response in listening to the book when I read it aloud as I always do with all my work.

R.G.

'Madame, why did your grandmother tell you to listen to the nightingale?'

'I think she was trying to tell me that, though I was a dancer first and foremost, there are still other things in the world that I should need.'

'What sort of things?'

'Oh, cats and dogs, flowers, books, parties, wine and people, of course.'

All things that were far out of the little dancer Lottie's reach.

R.G.

# LIST OF CHARACTERS

Prince, *a Cavalier King Charles spaniel*
Charlotte Tew (*Lottie*)
Auntie (*Miss Aimée/Amy Tew*)
Salvatore Ruffino
Domenico Ruffino, *Salvatore's papa*
Violetta, *his sister*
Sam, *the Ruffinos' chauffeur*
Serafina, *their housekeeper*

## VERBENA ROAD

Miss Dorcas and Miss Dora
(*their budgerigars, Sylvie and Victor*)
Mr Soper, *landlord*
Mrs Cuthbert (*Edna*)

## HOLBEIN'S

Madame Anna Holbein
Zanny, *her one-time dresser*
Emil Zanny's husband, *caretaker of the theatre*
Hilda Frost/Lionel Ray, *dancers in the Holbein Company*
Gregor Gustave, *Impresario*
Zoë/Archie, *children at Holbein's*

PANEL FOR HER MAJESTY'S BALLET, JUNIOR
SCHOOL, QUEEN'S CHASE AUDITION
Ennis Glyn, *director of senior and junior schools*
Elizabeth Baxter, *principal of senior and junior schools*
Jean McKenzie, *senior ballet mistress at Queen's Chase*

AT THE AUDITION
Irene St Charles, *Lottie's contemporary*
Mr and Mrs St Charles

QUEEN'S CHASE
HOUSEHOLD STAFF
Mrs Challoner, *headmistress of Queen's Chase School*
Daphne Layton, *her secretary*
Mr Ormond, *boys' housemaster*
Polly Walsh, *boys' matron*
Mrs Gillespie, *housemistress*
Sister
Mrs Meredith, *housekeeper/caterer*
Chef
Mr Lydd, *handyman*
Dr Paul, *the doctor*
Mrs Robinson

BALLET
Miss McKenzie, *senior ballet mistress*
Mr Max, *senior ballet master*
Miss Hurley, *the oldest teacher*
Mamzelly (Mlle Giroux), *teacher*
Mr Belton

Jonah Templeton, *accompanist*
Angela, *fourth-year girl*
John, *fourth-year boy*
Charles, *fourth-year boy*
Jake, *fourth-year boy*
Pamela, *second-year girl*

FIRST-YEAR PUPILS
Priscilla
Desmond
John
Thomas
Anne-Marie
Sybil
Abigail

Geoffrey Pick, *choreographer to*
Her Majesty's Ballet Company
Shaun Donaghue, *principal in the Company*
Mr Adams, *an animal trainer*

# CHAPTER I

She saw him and he saw her.

She, ten-year-old Lottie, was standing with her case on the kerb of a narrow London street. He was a puppy in a pet shop looking at her through a plate-glass window. Every time Lottie came this way she stopped to gaze at the pet shop while the traffic of the main road roared and stopped and roared again beside her. If only I could have a guinea pig or hamster ... but to Auntie, Lottie's aunt, guinea pigs and hamsters were vermin and she was horrified by them. Lottie could not have a kitten because of the budgerigars kept by the two old ladies, twins, Miss Dorcas and Miss Dora. Lottie had not thought of a puppy but then she had not seen this puppy before, small, silken white with chestnut-coloured markings; his ears, chestnut too, hung down each side of his earnest little face, white with chestnut round the eyes which were dark and

1

sparkling with interest. She looked at him, he looked at her and it was as if an invisible thread stretched across the street and tied them together, tight.

Though she knew she ought to, Lottie did not go away; instead she put her case down on the pavement and sat on it. 'Never let it out of your sight,' Auntie had taught her. 'Someone might snatch it.' Auntie always feared the worst, but, They can't snatch it if I'm sitting on it, thought Lottie as she looked yearningly across at the pet shop and the puppy.

In the case was a clean, carefully folded leotard and a brush and comb, because that afternoon she was on her way, or should have been on her way, to be photographed: 'Back and front and sides,' Auntie had instructed her, 'in your leotard, your plaits up on the top of your head, no wisps. Arms down by your sides, remember, bare feet.' Mr Winston, official photographer to the Holbein Theatre, had offered to take them. 'I couldn't refuse,' said Auntie, 'but I hope he doesn't charge too much.' The photograph was important; copies had to be sent with the form applying for a special audition being held by Her Majesty's Ballet, for a place, that very autumn term, in its junior ballet school, Queen's Chase.

'Queen's Chase? That's in Buckingham Park. It's a boarding school.'

Mrs Cuthbert, who was officially Auntie's best friend, liked to know all their business. 'How are you going to pay for that, Amy?' Mrs Cuthbert, who was also their near neighbour, called Auntie 'Amy' though Auntie took pride in being 'Aimée'. Why shouldn't she be Aimée if she wants to? thought rebellious Lottie. 'Queen's Chase is the ballet's boarding school. How will you pay for that?'

'They pay for everything.' For a moment Auntie's eyes shone. 'Even shoes.'

Shoes were Auntie's and Lottie's nightmare; even the regulation dancing shoes for girls, soft pale pink satin, were expensive and soon wore out. 'If only you were a boy and could have kid leather ones,' Auntie always lamented. 'Soon you'll be needing *pointe* shoes.'

'She gets a grant for her uniform,' Auntie was saying, '*if* she gets in but think, Edna. Every year three or four hundred children, maybe more, audition for Queen's Chase and perhaps twenty or fifteen get in. I don't suppose Lottie has a chance.'

'Why not?' Madame Holbein would have asked. Lottie would have asked that too. She knew that God – Auntie always emphasised that it was God – had given her, Lottie, a talent for dancing, and a strong, well-made slender little body to match. Holbein's had done the rest.

'Holbein's' meant Madame Anna Holbein's own ballet

3

school and small theatre in Hampstead where Auntie had worked in the wardrobe of the Company all her grown-up life.

Once upon a time – a hundred years ago the smallest children at Holbein's believed – Madame had been Niura, a little Russian girl living in the country with her grandmother. '"Niura," she used to tell me,' Madame in turn told the children, '"listen to the nightingale."'

'Why did she tell you to listen to the nightingale?' asked Archie, an inquisitive boy.

'I think she was trying to tell me that, though I was a dancer first and foremost, there are still other things in the world that I should need – yes, *need*,' said Madame.

'What sort of things?'

'Oh, cats and dogs, flowers, books, parties, wine and people, of course.' All things far removed from Lottie. 'We all need them and I have listened to nightingales and their kind ever since.'

Lottie wished she could hear a nightingale.

Madame's grandmother had taken Niura to the famous Imperial Theatre Ballet School in Petrograd – 'They call it Leningrad now,' said Auntie – and there Niura had turned into Anna Holbein, the famous ballerina. 'Ballerina! *Ballerina assoluta!*' said Auntie. It was a shock when Auntie learned that, in Her Majesty's Ballet and

4

other modern ballets, ballerinas were called, simply, principals.

After dancing all over the world, Anna Holbein had come to London where she had opened her own school and built up her Company in a big house in Hampstead. Its theatre had been the coach house which was hung with wisteria, grown so spreading that, 'There is not another like it in London,' said Madame. 'A perfect setting.' It was here that she gave her Seasons. Her theatre and her Company became renowned.

Perhaps Auntie expected the worst because that was what she had always had. She was so gentle and unassuming that she seemed born to be protected; instead it seemed she had to protect almost everyone else. Her father and mother had died when she was seventeen, leaving her with a little sister, eight-year-old Henrietta, who was already attending Holbein's classes. Though Auntie was so young, Madame, to help her, had taken her as an assistant in the wardrobe but Auntie was skilful and had quickly risen to be wardrobe mistress which meant not only keeping in repair but making many of the costumes, 'For a pittance,' Mrs Cuthbert had said.

It was true Madame did not pay much but, 'We manage,' said Auntie.

'You could get help with your rent and heating,' said Mrs Cuthbert.

'I prefer not,' said Auntie who was proud. She did take child benefit, but that was for Lottie, 'All the same I'd rather not have it,' said Auntie.

'Then you must ask Madame Holbein for a rise.'

'I couldn't do that.' Auntie had been shocked.

Auntie loved and revered Madame and Madame in her outspoken way did try to encourage her. 'You would be quite pretty', she told her, 'if you didn't strain your hair back and wear such dreary clothes.'

Auntie chose what she called serviceable clothes, old-fashioned dark grey or brown 'that won't show the dirt', but if there were any bits and pieces left over in the wardrobe she made Lottie gay little skirts and blouses. 'Madame has done everything for us,' she always said, besides she liked being Holbein's wardrobe mistress, treated with respect and called Miss Tew – Miss Tew could be as dictatorial and firm as Auntie was doubting and worried at home. Madame, too, had trained Henrietta, 'For free,' Auntie said but Henrietta had rewarded Madame by becoming the star of her Company – 'Star quality,' Madame had said – but, sadly, she had been as wilful and wild as she was talented and at the beginning of a brilliant career had died giving birth to a baby – Lottie. 'Leaving me to bring up a child all over again. Henrietta at least was eight. You were a baby,' said Auntie.

'But I must have had a father,' argued Lottie. 'I must have.'

'Yes.' Auntie spoke with strange reluctance.

'Then where is he? Who is he? Who?' and it came out.

'I don't know where he is. I don't know who he is. That's why you're called Charlotte Tew. We don't talk about it, Lottie. Remember that, but it's why things have been so difficult for us.'

'Your aunt worked her fingers to the bone for you,' Mrs Cuthbert liked to tell Lottie, but Lottie took comfort in that Auntie had plenty of fingers left, even if they were needle pricked.

Lottie had first come to Holbein's in a carry cot. When she was four she joined in the baby class not once or twice a week like the others but every day. At seven she had been promoted to a weekly class with Madame herself; Lottie was shy but she quickly ousted Zoë, a big showy child who, until then, had shown the greatest promise. Madame gave no sign of this but the class knew it to the last hair on their small heads.

'Madame only takes you because she's sorry for you,' Mrs Cuthbert told Lottie.

'Sorry for you!' Madame had said when Lottie asked her if that were true. '*Sorry* for you! When you are one of the luckiest girls in all Europe. How many', demanded Madame, 'have the body, the will, the strength and the talent to dance?'

'I know,' said Lottie. 'Auntie says I should go down on my knees every night and thank God for it.'

'It would be much better if you used your knees for what God intended them, to bend, to lift, and to stretch,' said Madame. 'Not like that weak, wobbly *developpé* you did for me just now.'

The more Madame valued pupils the more she execrated them; Lottie was often bewildered by the criticisms and reproofs that were poured on her when she knew she had listened to every word Madame said and obviously done the best *enchaînement* – a chain of simple steps. 'First you learn the steps, then you make little sentences,' Madame would say or more often, 'Ah, *bah*! What do you think is *that*?'

Her eyes were bright and darting as a witch's, her shoulders huddled in the old purple jacket she always wore. 'Does she sleep in it?' the children giggled.

'It's a disgrace,' said Auntie but Lottie could see nothing wrong with the jacket, it was the colour of pansies.

Lottie knew pansies, they grew in Holbein's garden. When summer comes I'll pick a bunch of them and give them to Madame. Lottie, though, was prudent. I'll wait till the others have gone home.

'Madame. I have a tiny little surprise for you.'

'For *me*?' Madame could always be counted on to respond. 'Just when I was wanting a few flowers!'

Lottie knew where Madame would put them: in her sitting room she had what she called an icon, a holy picture
of Mary and Jesus painted on wood in blues made from
lapis lazuli, enamels and gold, which was always lit by the
flame from a little red glass lamp she kept burning in front
of it. Often in moments of difficulty Lottie would creep
upstairs and look through the door to glimpse the light
and be cheered.

It never occurred to her that it could go out.

'Lottie. Lottie wake up!'

'Wake up. Why?' Lottie's eyes were still full of sleep.
Then Auntie's flood of tears alarmed her.

'They've just telephoned from Holbein's' – the telephone wasn't Auntie's, it was in the house hall – 'to tell
us.'

'Tell us what?'

'Lottie, Madame Holbein is dead.'

'Dead? Madame? She can't be.'

'She is. She died in the night.'

'No.' It was not possible. Madame was the pivot of
Lottie's and Auntie's beings. 'She wouldn't. She couldn't,'
but Madame had died.

'And I can guess this will be the end of your dancing,'
Mrs Cuthbert had said.

Mrs Cuthbert, though, had not counted on Madame.

True, Holbein's was stricken but only until Hilda came. Hilda had heard the news in Austria where she was dancing, cancelled her engagements and had come at once to help.

Hilda was Hilda Frost, Madame's latest triumph, a jewel of a dancer, polished as a precious stone and also one of those rare beings, a choreographer as well. She had already done two ballets for Madame, both promising, and sometimes, between engagements, she was trusted to take Madame's classes. 'But Madame never liked her,' said Auntie. 'They are too alike.' Madame's love was for Lionel Ray, Hilda's partner, a magnificent young male dancer whom everyone called Lion. He, like Henrietta and Lottie, had been taken for nothing when he was a boy and had become for Madame like her own son. 'She'll leave Holbein's to him,' everyone was sure but, no, Madame left Holbein's to Hilda, 'Because she is the only one I can trust.'

Hilda loved the little theatre passionately. 'Of course the Company will go on,' she vowed. She had to close the school but there was not a child whose future she did not try to arrange. Lottie, though, was the only one she chose to apply for a place at Queen's Chase. 'By great luck there is to be a special audition this month as one of the girls and one of the boys have fallen out.'

Most boys and girls, if they are serious dancers, pester

their fathers and mothers to let them try for a place at Queen's Chase; no one had even asked Lottie. It was taken as settled which was why now she was on her way to the photographer – or should have been; instead, she was sitting on her case gazing at the puppy in the window.

Suddenly she stiffened. Then jumped to her feet.

She had noticed a big boy standing by the pet-shop door, a boy of at least sixteen wearing jeans and a loose sloppy jersey. He had been looking intently into the pet shop – the door was open and Lottie could see into it too. Beyond the low partition that shut off the puppy pen in the window she could see tiers of cages of small animals and birds, glass tanks of fish, baskets stacked, a rack of leads and collars. A lady in a pink overall was showing a white rabbit to a little boy and a gentleman; they had their backs to the door. As Lottie watched the big boy sidled nearer, then, quick as a flash, darted in, picked up a puppy by the scruff of its neck – *the* puppy – put it under his jersey and was gone whistling as he sauntered up the street.

But the pet-shop lady had seen. She rushed to the door calling, 'Stop him! Thief! Thief! Police! Police!' The boy dodged across the road and started to run. Without stopping to think Lottie picked up her case and ran after him.

A dancer is a good athlete and Lottie ran fast, came abreast of the boy and flung her case in front of him. Sure enough he tripped and fell, the puppy underneath him. There were piercing little animal shrieks as the puppy rolled out of the jersey and into the gutter. Lottie snatched him up and held him still shrieking. He was warm and squirming in her arms; she had never held anything as small and warm and precious.

'I saw.' A lady was standing beside her. 'Snatched your pet, did he? The big lout.'

'No, no,' but Lottie was too out of breath to say it and as the puppy's cries went on she started to cry.

'Blasted young hooligan! He nearly knocked me over. Broad daylight too! A child's puppy!'

'He's hurt. He's dying,' Lottie sobbed.

'If he was dying he wouldn't be squealing.' The lady seemed to know about puppies. 'You saved him. I must say you were a right smart girl to throw your case.'

'I'm not,' said Lottie, still sobbing.

'Never mind, you've got him safe. Tell you what. There's a People's Dispensary for Sick Animals in the next street. We'll take him there.'

'Oh, you are kind.'

'There! There! I'll take your case. Come, love,' and Lottie carried the adorable weight of the puppy, her tears dropping on his head as the shrieks turned to pitiful moans.

Lottie did not have to explain to the vet, the kind lady

did it for her but not as it had really been. 'Poor mite. She was walking her puppy—'

'I wasn't,' Lottie began but the kind lady swept on.

'Broad daylight. What's the world coming to if a child can't do that? One of them skinheads or whatever they call themselves. The police shut their eyes—'

The vet in his white coat interrupted her. 'Let me look at him.' He took the puppy from Lottie and laid him on the table where his tail immediately began to wag.

'There now,' said the kind lady. 'I told you he wasn't badly hurt, and what a beautiful little dog he is, sir, isn't he? But what is he?'

'A Cavalier King Charles spaniel,' but the vet was frowning. 'He hasn't got a collar on. Don't you know,' he said severely to Lottie, 'you should never take a dog, even a puppy in a London street – or any street – without a collar and lead?'

'He hasn't got a collar yet,' said Lottie, and to her surprise, she added, 'he's new.'

'Well, get him one.' The vet was examining the puppy. 'Fell right on top of him?' and he said to the puppy, 'You're a lucky little fellow. Not even winded. No bones broken. He'll be a bit bruised and sore for a few days. Take him home, give him some warm milk with sugar in it and keep him quiet.'

'Take him home. The vet told me to do that,' Lottie

argued with herself though she knew it was cheating. 'You take him straight back to the pet shop,' Lottie told Lottie, but the vet had put him into her arms where he snuggled and a little tongue came out and licked her face.

'I must say he's a little beauty,' said the kind lady. 'What's his name?'

'Prince.' Mysteriously that was his name because, He's royal, thought Lottie and, 'I can't. I can't,' she said to the pet shop and had to argue with herself, 'Why should I have been there on the pavement just at that moment?' and she told herself something Auntie often said, 'It was meant.'

'Well, all's well that ends well,' the kind lady said when they were out in the street. 'Will you be all right, love? I expect you live round here.'

Lottie did not tell her she lived in Hampstead, quite a journey by bus or underground. Instead, 'I must buy him a collar and lead first.'

The vet had said that too. Lottie had a ten-pound note in her case – it was for the photographer but she had forgotten about the photographs – and she had said to the vet as Auntie always said about a bill, 'What do I owe you?'

'Nothing,' said the vet. 'I did nothing but don't take him out again without a collar and a lead.'

'A collar and lead.'

'Woolworth's,' said the kind lady promptly. Lottie had

been afraid she would say the pet shop. 'Woolworth's is on my way. I'll show you.'

They found a green collar and lead that set off Prince's colouring. It had a little metal tag. 'You must have your name and address on that,' which gave Lottie such a surge of joy that she forgot all about the pet shop. They found a drinking bowl that had DOG on it: the kind lady was an enthusiastic shopper.

'Have you enough puppy food?' They bought a bag of puppy biscuits and some tins. 'You'll need lots of newspapers.'

'Newspapers? What for?'

'Toilet training,' said the lady. Lottie had not thought of that. 'Teach him to go on a newspaper. He'll soon learn. Do you look after him all yourself, dearie? That's a lot for a little girl. Puppies are as demanding as babies,' and she asked, 'Has he a toy, something to play with?' and, as Lottie shook her head – she did not know puppies had toys – 'An old slipper?'

'All our slippers are old,' Lottie could have said, but the kind lady rushed on, 'Look, we'll buy him a ball.'

By the time they had finished Lottie's head was reeling and half the ten pounds was gone but the sales girl had said, 'That's a lovely little puppy you have there.'

'Pedigree,' said the kind lady, a word Lottie had not heard before.

'However are you going to get all this and little Prince home?'

That was a question. I can't take him on the underground, thought Lottie. They might not allow him on a bus. In any case I can't carry all this. She must have been 'out of herself' as Mrs Cuthbert often told her she was, because she took a deep breath and said what she and Auntie had never said in their lives. 'I'll take a taxi.'

# CHAPTER II

Home for Lottie and Auntie was the basement flat of Mr Soper's Victorian villa, number 5 Verbena Road in Hampstead.

Mr Soper himself lived on the first floor. Miss Dorcas and Miss Dora had the top flat and the attic where they kept their budgerigars.

Though the basement was dismal and cold, the sitting room looked on the garden as did Lottie's bedroom – it was typical of Auntie to give the best room first to Henrietta, then to Lottie. The carpets were threadbare, the walls dingy but the sitting room held two things dear to Auntie's heart: an open fireplace where they lit a fire on Sundays and on special occasions – the warm flickering light transformed the room – and also a cabinet where she kept her treasures: a Dresden china shepherdess, a miniature tea-set and a pair of Staffordshire dogs that had belonged to the family. 'Never forget, Lottie, that though we may be badly off, the Tews come from a *good* family – we are distant cousins of Lord Wamphrey.' More importantly than even the Staffordshire dogs, the cabinet held Henrietta's first *pointe* shoes, a white lace fan she had used, a locket with her hair, her make-up box with its pots of rouge and colours and its hare-foot brush. 'One day that box will be yours,' Auntie told Lottie reverently.

In all the years Lottie had lived there no taxi had ever stopped at number 5 Verbena Road. Though they had their separate door bells, the tenants all shared the hall – Auntie and Lottie had steps leading down to the basement – and, as the kind taxi-man helped Lottie into the hall with the packages while Prince, who was not used to wearing any kind of harness, twisted on his collar and lead like a fish on the end of a line, she saw two white heads pop over the banisters far above, while Mr Soper came to his door. Prince chose that moment to squat and make a large puddle on the hall carpet. 'Tchk! Tchk!' sounded from above, as, Newspapers, newspapers, thought Lottie frantically. I must get newspapers, but how? She worried until, Mr Soper will have them, she thought.

\*

'Mr Soper. Mr Soaker,' said Mrs Cuthbert. It was true that Mr Soper drank – his dustbin was full of empty wine bottles – but he was always kind and courteous to Auntie and Lottie.

Miss Dorcas and Miss Dora were so alike that it was almost impossible to tell them apart, except that Miss Dorcas's eyes were bluer, she was the least bit larger and she always spoke first, Miss Dora echoing her. They had not been parted, even for one night, since they were born, and seemed to need no one but each other though they admitted Lottie. 'Sister,' Miss Dorcas had once said, 'if we had to go into hospital or anywhere, Lottie would look after our birds.'

'She could look after our budgies.'

The budgerigars were kept in the attic. 'Unhygienic,' said Mrs Cuthbert. 'Bird droppings and grain. It'll bring rats.'

'Oh, Edna! Do you think so?' Auntie had an almost morbid dread of rats but to Lottie the attic's big aviary, where blue-, green- and yellow-feathered birds flew and perched, was like a glimpse of heaven. On Sunday mornings she was allowed to help to clean the aviary and even take out the two favourites, Victor and Sylvie, perched on her finger.

The 'tchks' now were gentle and Lottie knew that, though Mr Soper, Miss Dorcas and Miss Dora were interested and curious, none of them would have dreamt of coming into the hall or of asking questions, or interfering and she was grateful because, 'We mustn't talk to anyone, anyone at all,' Lottie told Prince, 'until Auntie has seen you. Prince, if only, only you can make her like you!'

Lottie made careful preparations. She unpacked Prince's drinking bowl, opened a tin and fed him, then took him into the garden where he went wild with delight even with his bruises – That's after being shut in a pen, thought Lottie. He rushed round and round, pouncing and running until suddenly he stopped, yawned, keeled over and fell into a deep puppy sleep. Lottie gathered him up with a tenderness that she had never known before and carried him inside. For sleeping she had found a large carton in the back hall – Mr Soper never threw anything away. 'I wish I could have bought you one of those lovely baskets,' she told Prince, 'but this will have to do for now.' Prince did not seem to mind but curled up on a jersey that was too old for even Lottie to wear. Asleep, Prince was even more endearing than when he was awake; he looked so warm, small and help-less. She put the carton into her bedroom and shut the door.

She lit the fire – it was a sort of celebration day. She scented it with pine cones she had picked up on the Heath, then laid the table with tea things ready.

When Hilda had told her about Queen's Chase, Lottie had objected, 'Auntie couldn't manage without me.'

Hilda had answered, 'She must, Lottie. Never let anyone, or anything, come between you and your dancing.'

'Of course I can manage,' said Auntie. 'Haven't I always?' but Lottie was a much better manager than Auntie.

'I said Special Offer,' she would say sternly in the corner shop where Auntie insisted on going – 'Because it has been there always and they're like friends.'

'They would still try and sell you the most expensive butter,' said Lottie.

Mrs Cuthbert, too, could make Auntie do what Auntie did not want to do, like buying the television.

Much as Lottie would have liked a television she did not want Auntie bullied into having one; if Auntie protected Lottie, Lottie had grown to protect Auntie, but Mrs Cuthbert was strong.

'Everyone has one, Amy. It's part of every day.'

'I don't know when we'd have the time to look at it.'

'Then it's time you did, you can watch while you sew.'

'Never! My sewing needs all my attention. I couldn't watch and sew, and Lottie has her homework and practising.'

'Weekends. Holidays.'

'No, Edna,' but Auntie bought a television on hire purchase terms, then lay awake wondering how she could pay the next instalment. 'They'll take it away and we'll lose all that good money.'

Now Lottie peeled potatoes and set them boiling; she had a small packet of frozen peas and two cutlets ready to grill; there was the last of Sunday's sponge cake. Everything was ready for a tired Auntie and, I won't show her Prince at once. Let her arrange herself first, putting down the heavy carrier bags of sewing she always brought home.

Then her umbrella would be put away – Auntie took an umbrella wet or fine; she would hang up her coat, putting her gloves in the pocket. She would take off her shoes with a sigh of relief, put on slippers, not bedroom slippers, light embroidered ones, and go into her bedroom to wash her hands and tidy her hair before she said, 'Love, put the kettle on.'

That was how it should have gone tonight, Tea first, Lottie had thought. It was Prince who upset her plans.

As soon as Auntie opened the front door, he woke. 'He's going to make an excellent watch dog,' Mr Soper was to say. There was a frantic scratching. 'What's that?' Auntie paused. She had put down her bags and was yielding Lottie her umbrella.

'What's that? Rats?'

'Auntie, give me your coat.'

'Lottie!' Auntie started back in horror. 'It *is* rats! I knew it.'

'It isn't rats, Auntie. Come to the fire. Sit down,' commanded Lottie. 'Now look,' and she opened her bedroom door.

'Lottie!' It was almost as shrill as for the rats. 'Whatever on earth is that?' Then, 'Lottie! What is it?'

Prince answered for himself. He trotted over, sniffed Auntie's slippers and skirt, then lifted himself up against her knee. Auntie shrank but, as he lifted, too, that enquiring paw, looking innocently up into her face, his chestnut ears hanging down, she put out her hand and touched his head.

'It's like silk,' she whispered – Auntie always recognised quality. 'What a little beauty!'

'Isn't he? His name's Prince. He's a Cavalier King Charles spaniel.' Lottie lingered over his name.

'But how? What? Where?' asked Auntie in bewilderment.

'I … picked him up.' That was true. 'He was in the street.' True too. 'No one seemed to know anything about him.' There had been no one to know except, 'A kind lady helped me,' who had not known either – or only half of it. 'We bought him a collar and lead at Woolworth's and I brought him home.' She was interrupted.

Lottie had just time to remove Prince and put him on a newspaper before he made a puddle. Auntie laughed. It was a long time since Auntie had laughed. 'Where did you learn to do that with the newspaper?'

'The kind lady told me. You see, he's trained,' Lottie said in triumph.

But it was not all as easy: 'Mr Soper, have you any more newspapers?'

'What, already?' asked Mr Soper.

'A puppy is as demanding as a baby,' the kind lady had told Lottie and, 'Auntie, when I was a baby did I cry in the night?' Lottie asked.

'Day and night,' said Auntie.

Prince had cried so much that Lottie had had to sleep with one hand in his basket, which meant, when finally she did get to sleep herself, she woke late and he was awash. When she had taken him in the garden, even though it was nearly seven o'clock, his delighted barks had made several of the neighbours push up their windows indignantly. 'I shall have to get up at six and take you in the street,' she told Prince which was a dismal prospect.

Then, at breakfast, Auntie began asking questions – sense was beginning to break through.

'How can we feed him?'

Lottie evaded that. 'Scraps,' she said, though she knew

they seldom had scraps. 'He can have half my milk. I'm too big for milk.'

It was when Lottie was washing up while Auntie tidied the flat that Auntie suddenly asked, 'What about the photographs?'

Crash went a plate. The photographs! Prince had wiped every thought of the photographs out of Lottie's mind.

'They're – they're coming,' she said, yet she did not see how they could and, straight away, on remembering the photographs, she remembered something even more dreadful, the ten-pound note. Ten pounds! How could I? Lottie's hands were shaking as she gathered up the bits of broken china.

'You haven't given me the change,' Auntie went on.

'I . . . I'll need some of it for shopping.'

'Well, keep a careful account.' Auntie had her coat on. 'Dear me. I'll be late.' It was only as she picked up her gloves, umbrella and bags that she stopped. 'Lottie! The little dog, Prince! What are you going to do with Prince? You can't leave him alone all day and you can't take him to school,' and, as full realisation dawned, 'Oh, Lottie! What have you been and gone and *done?*'

# CHAPTER III

What Lottie had not told Auntie was that she was not going to school, 'Not today. How can I?' she would have said. 'I must arrange things. I'll stay away today, then tomorrow I'll come back at break time and see to Prince.' School was only up the hill but, I'll have to run, thought Lottie. I'll have my dinner, she knew school dinners were a great relief to Auntie. But I'll take a plastic bag, hide it in my school case, choose the plainest, meatiest food, eat half as quickly as I can, keep the other half for Prince, come home and feed him. We have an hour. There'll be plenty of time. Meanwhile there were urgent things to do.

First of all, ten pounds and the photographs: she had to get them, and today.

Lottie was quite used to doing things on her own. Since she was eight she had done Auntie's errands after school, going down to London's West End by bus or underground chiefly to what they called the bead shop which sold buckles and sequins as well as ribbons, fringes and gauzy net, or to the button shop that sold only buttons, or to shops where she had to bring back patterns of fabrics. Sometimes she carried quite a sum of money. 'No one's going to notice a little schoolgirl,' Auntie comforted herself, but Lottie always had a note from Auntie: 'Please allow my niece ...' and signed, 'Aimée Tew, Wardrobe Mistress, Holbein Theatre.' Now Lottie had even more complicated things to do quite by herself.

There was only one way out for the ten pounds and, slowly, unwillingly, she went to Auntie's desk and opened the drawer where her, Lottie's, post-office savings book was kept, money saved, if not penny by penny, ten pence by ten pence since she was two years old. 'Not to spend,' Auntie always said. 'One day you'll need it. Even if you get in to Queen's Chase, we can't let them pay for everything. You haven't a suitcase and you have to have a *cloak*!' That, to Auntie, seemed a wanton extravagance for a small girl, yet a matter of pride. Now, as Lottie picked up the little blue book, she felt she was cheating Auntie. But I have to. I must, she thought. I must take out ten pounds.

She also had to take a note from Auntie. I'll have to write it myself. Luckily, in her coat pocket, she had one of such notes, 'Please allow my niece to ...' Lottie knew she could not spell and, on a sheet of Holbein's headed writing paper, she copied: 'To whom it may concern. Please allow my niece, Charlotte Tew, to cash ten pounds from her post-office savings book' – that was printed on it – and Lottie carefully traced Auntie's signature. She seemed to go from one bad thing to another.

She took Prince to the post office which meant delays.

'*What* an adorable puppy!'

'What's his name?'

'Where did you get him?'

'Buckingham Palace,' said Lottie, which was pert but she was in a hurry. She knew what to do at the post office, she had often been there but always to put a little money in, never to take it out. By the time she got back to the flat, it was nearly eleven. She could not take Prince to the photographer, so she bundled him into his box, and put newspapers all over the floor – luckily he was tired and went to sleep. She forgot her case which had her leotard in it and had to go back, then ran all the way to the underground station. Mr Winston was not pleased. 'Your appointment was for yesterday, *and* in the afternoon.'

'I was on my way to keep it,' Lottie told him, 'but I was unavoidably detained.' That was how Auntie made excuses.

Mr Winston photographed Lottie, back and front and sides in her leotard, her plaits upon the top of her head, her feet bare. It took ages and ages, and Lottie was in agony, but Mr Winston, too, was kind. He gave Lottie back the ten pounds, 'I couldn't think of taking that from Miss Tew,' flooding Lottie with relief. *Now I can put it back in my savings book – Auntie need never know, but I shall have to go to the post office again.*

Then on the way back she needed to stop and shop; by the time she got home she was as frantic as Prince. He had made two puddles dutifully on the newspaper but another just by his box. 'That's naughty,' Lottie scolded and, naughtier still, yet another in the sitting room before she could get him into the garden. She watched him as he lapped up the milk she longed for – she had crumbled a slice of bread into it keeping the crust for herself – Lottie had to admit that a puppy, even the most adorable one in the whole world, cost far more than money.

'You managed,' said Auntie that evening with satisfaction.

'Just.' Lottie was not telling Auntie any more than that.

'So it's true,' said Mrs Cuthbert. 'I met Mr Soper in the road and he told me Lottie had a little dog. Where did you get him?'

'Lottie found him,' said Auntie.

'Where?'

'In the street,' Lottie had to say.

'*Found* him in the *street?*'

'Yes.' Lottie did not intend to say more than that, but Mrs Cuthbert went on.

'No one about?'

'There was a kind lady,' Lottie had to admit.

'You should have asked at the houses.'

'We did ask the vet.'

'What vet?'

'Prince – the puppy – was hurt. The lady helped me take him to the vet.'

'You should have taken it to the police station.'

'The police!' That gave Lottie a shock.

'Good gracious, Lottie, it's time you were in bed.' Auntie had seen the shock. 'You take Prince in the garden and then off with you both. Aunt Edna and I will have a cup of tea.' 'Aunt Edna' was to mollify Mrs Cuthbert. 'Look, Edna. These are the forms for the audition. You might be interested to see—'

'I see.' Mrs Cuthbert pushed the forms aside. 'Amy, I see only too clearly. Lottie has a little dog. How does looking after a little dog go with all this dancing, Miss, *if* I may ask?'

'Not very well,' would have been the truthful answer.

Though Lottie had missed school that day there was something she could not miss: Hilda's class at Holbein's.

Overworked as Hilda was, she had set apart an hour every afternoon, 'Until the audition,' to coach the three remaining children, Zoë, Archie and Lottie, but the class was really for Lottie and Lottie knew it. Sometimes Hilda had to keep them waiting, sometimes she cut them short, but she was always faithful. 'It's *so* good of Hilda.' Auntie was full of admiration. 'I hope you appreciate it, Lottie.'

'Not always,' Lottie could have said.

Prince had cried so piteously when she had left him at three o'clock that she seemed to hear him through the music; then he had begun to yap which was worse. The neighbours will hear him ... 'Lottie, you're not paying attention,' said Hilda.

A few minutes later. 'Lottie, didn't you hear me?'

'I'm sorry, Hilda,' but Hilda's sharp clap stopped the pianist again.

'Lottie, will you please tell me the *enchaînement* I've just set you.'

'Starting right foot, three *jetés, temps levés*,' Lottie began uncertainly.

'Yes?'

'*Glissade derrière* towards left and *pas de basque*—'

'*Pas de basque?*' Hilda almost screamed and Zoë's hand shot up.

'*Glissade derrière, pas de chat*,' said glib Zoë.

'Evidently Lottie has never heard of a *pas de chat*,' said Hilda in withering sarcasm. 'They *will* think a lot of her at Queen's Chase!'

'If she gets in,' Zoë and Archie sniggered.

If only, thought Lottie that evening in the garden where she had escaped with Prince. If only Auntie and I were the only people in the world! In fairness she had to add Mr Soper, Miss Dorcas and Miss Dora.

Lottie had introduced Prince to Mr Soper when she had asked him about the newspapers. 'Splendid little chap!' Mr Soper had said and not a word about tenants not keeping dogs. Prince had met Miss Dorcas and Miss Dora in the hall.

'*What* a little darling!' Miss Dorcas had cried.

'Darling!' cried Miss Dora.

'Pretty fellow!'

'So, so pretty.'

They had patted and petted Prince and only said, 'Better not let him upstairs, dearie, because of the budgies.' Now the sitting-room window was open and Lottie could not help overhearing Mrs Cuthbert's loud voice, 'Mark my words, Amy, no good will come of that dog. Take it to the police before she becomes too attached.'

'She is attached,' said Auntie helplessly.

Attached! Lottie lived for Prince. Faithfully, she dragged herself out of bed at six o'clock each morning; a gleam of joy was that Prince rewarded her in the street almost at once – he was a remarkably intelligent puppy – but everything was complicated by her having to go to school. The people who lived in Verbena Road grew quite accustomed to see her flying past, her plaits and school-bag flying too, as she hurtled along the pavement, up or down it, six times a day.

She tore home at break, back to school almost at once, gobbled half of her dinner so fast she almost choked, ran with the rest to Prince, spent a brief time with him in the garden, then back to school and another run home before it was time to run again to Holbein's.

There were consolations. Saturday was a respite: though there was housework and shopping – Auntie worked on Saturdays – there was no school and Lottie took Prince up on Hampstead Heath, carrying him up the hill. 'Puppies shouldn't walk too far,' the kind lady had told her. Lottie loved the Heath; the pond where proud men, as well as boys, sailed or steamed their model boats and a woman sold balloons. She liked to walk over the grass and sit under a tree watching the world go by. She found a tree now and let Prince off the lead. He was tired, sat beside her and soon, puppy-wise, went to sleep.

A car drew up on the edge of the road, a big shining car, dark green; a chauffeur got out, he had a dark green uniform to match the car. He opened the door of the passenger seat and said in a coaxing voice, 'Violetta, come. Come, get out for a little.'

There was a woman in the back of the car and she too spoke volubly in a foreign language. Then, 'Come on, Vivi,' said the young chauffeur. 'You're going to do a little walk for Sam.'

'No. Io ti dico, *no*! I told you no.'

'Come on, Princess' – perhaps she really is a princess, thought Lottie – but the chauffeur had reached in and lifted the little girl bodily out.

Children can't do anything against grown-ups, thought Lottie with a surge of indignation but it seemed this child could. Violetta, or Vivi, screamed and hit out at Sam. 'No. No, ci sono troppo persone – too many people. They'll look at me. You know they will.'

The woman joined in expostulating, whether with the chauffeur or the little girl Lottie could not tell but it was a stream of foreign talk, Italian, thought Lottie who had often heard Italian at Holbein's. There was going to be a scene but the voice had woken Prince and before Lottie could catch him he had run over the grass to the car.

'Prince! Come back.' Lottie ran after him and, as he jumped round the little girl, 'Down. Prince, *down*.'

The cries broke off at once as she tried to catch him. 'Oh! Oh!' she cried.

'Down, Prince. Down.' Lottie was afraid he would dirty the child's coat.

'Not down,' said the imperious little voice. 'Lui mi piace. I like him. Let him.'

The woman came out of the car and put out an anxious hand but Violetta had picked Prince up and was hugging him crooning, 'Che bel cagnolino! Beautiful little dog.'

She was not like any little girl Lottie had seen. She had auburn hair beautifully brushed – I thought Italians were dark, I didn't know they could have red hair, thought Lottie. It was too much hair for the wan little face where the eyes looked too large, violet eyes that matched Violetta's name. Most girls Lottie knew wore anoraks and jeans when they were not at school but Violetta was dressed like pictures Lottie had seen of the Queen and her sister when they were little girls, a blue tailored coat with a velvet collar and buttons, white socks – no wonder people look at her, thought Lottie – except that she had white leather boots and one leg was in a steel brace.

It was then that Sam the chauffeur said, 'I wonder if little Miss here would let you take the puppy for a walk.'

'Here's his lead,' said Lottie and Violetta watched in ecstasy while Lottie fastened him, then put the lead into her hand.

'Sam, she'll fall,' the woman was agitating but, 'Go away.' Violetta was passionate. 'Va via!'

'Give her your hand,' Sam whispered to Lottie who took Violetta's other hand. She was not steady, the leg with the brace made her limp but she walked to the tree and round the tree never noticing her leg and laughing when Prince twisted on his lead.

'Prince, behave,' Lottie told him but, 'No behave,' said Violetta laughing still more.

'Never, never talk to strangers,' Auntie had brought Lottie up to that but these were different; when Violetta had walked, never noticing the people, Sam brought a rug from the car and they all sat down under the tree except Sam who took off his chauffeur's hat and stretched out on the grass. 'Papa will be *so* pleased,' said the woman whose name it seemed was Serafina. She looked after Violetta. 'And the house,' said Serafina, 'because no mother. *Poverina.*' She had a hairbrush in her bag and began to brush Violetta's hair but Violetta twisted away. 'Basta! Lasciami *sola*. Leave me *alone*.' There was something piteous in that. Well I'd hate to have my hair brushed in front of people, thought Lottie, and she sensed, for all the prettiness, there was a small volcano in Violetta that let out puffs of smoke as a warning that it might erupt at any moment.

Serafina also held a small pair of white gloves. Lottie had

not known children wore gloves except in winter; she was to discover that it was Serafina, a dear devoted peasant woman, who dressed Violetta in the way she thought well-to-do children should be dressed. Even on that first afternoon Lottie could not help thinking they must be very rich, though Auntie said you must never be curious about other people's money; the car, Sam's uniform, even the pearls that Lottie was sure were real pearls in Violetta's miniature ear studs – her ears were pierced – all showed it, but being rich did not seem to make her a happy child.

She was happy now.

'A Cavalier King Charles spaniel!' She said that over and over again as if it were magic and Lottie had never seen anything as lovely as her little face flushed with delight. Sam whistled as he lay – he's happy too, for her, thought Lottie.

Soon it was time to go. 'Or you take a chill,' Serafina warned Violetta.

'You must come tomorrow,' Violetta told Lottie. 'Tu devi venire! You must come.'

Tomorrow was Sunday. 'Yes, I'll come,' said Lottie.

'I'll carry you to the car,' Sam offered.

'I can walk,' said Violetta who half an hour before had said she would not walk. 'Vatienne. Go away,' she told Sam. 'I'll walk with Lottie,' and as the car drove away, 'Ciao, bello,' she called.

Next day she came alone with Sam. 'Serafina fusses,' and indeed Serafina had fussed.

'Poor Serafina,' said Lottie, 'doesn't she like to get out on the Heath?'

'She like but I don't like.' Violetta said it as if that settled it.

Lottie had never heard a child talk to grown-up people in the way Violetta spoke to Sam and Serafina. Doesn't anyone ever tell her things? thought Lottie. She really must be a princess. Sam drove Lottie and Prince home. Like the taxi, such an opulent car had never stopped at number 5 Verbena Road, and stayed outside because Auntie asked Violetta and Sam in for tea – 'Fortunately as it is Sunday we have a sponge cake.' Auntie was entranced by Violetta who seemed to reign in the sitting room. Auntie was full of pity too. 'Poor little mite,' she whispered though 'poor' Lottie thought was not the right word.

'There was an accident when she was a baby,' Sam whispered back to Auntie. And Violetta was not a princess. Her surname was Ruffino and Mr Ruffino, Papa, had a successful delicatessen shop and a restaurant in Soho where they lived.

'Many Italians do,' said Auntie.

'It's not much of a life for Vivi,' said Sam.

Auntie was moved to make drop scones, which she hardly ever did but at the sight of the tea-table Violetta's face had grown mutinous. 'I have a problem,' she said to Auntie. 'I won't eat.'

Auntie gave one look at her – and at Sam who was embarrassed. 'Plenty of people don't eat,' said Auntie. 'You eat what you like, dearie, and leave the rest.'

Violetta was so used to being coaxed: 'Try and eat it up, cara', 'Just a little more', 'One more spoonful', that she stared at Auntie almost in rebuke but Auntie only said, 'Would you like to help me make scones for the others while Lottie opens the raspberry jam?' and she let an enchanted Violetta stand on a stool by the cooker and drop the mixture on to a hot girdle where it changed into a flat golden-brown scone. Violetta ate three and a slice of sponge cake while Sam marvelled.

Lottie noticed Violetta did not say, '*Grazie*,' thank you, when Auntie offered her a scone. Doesn't anyone teach her anything? she wondered again. Then, 'You must come tomorrow,' Violetta pleaded as Lottie took a sleepy Prince from her: though she said 'must' it was a plea not a command – there was something truly sweet about her when she was gentle – then she added, 'Per piacere – please,' but Lottie had to say, 'No.'

Violetta was not used to 'no'. She started to quiver but Auntie said swiftly, 'Lottie has things of her own she must do, Violetta,' and there was not as much as a puff of smoke.

'I'll come on Saturday. Sunday too.' Violetta put her arms round Lottie and hugged her.

'Bless you,' said Sam.

Lottie managed for two more weekdays but after school on the second day she was due to go to Holbein's.

'Lottie! Am I speaking double Dutch? I'm not going to tell you again.'

'I'm sorry, Hilda. I . . . I think perhaps I'm tired.'

'*You*'re tired,' snapped Hilda. 'What do you think I am?'

For Hilda the audition could not have come at a worse time. It was to be held on 13 September; the autumn term at Queen's Chase began on the nineteenth – Lottie's state school had already gone back – and, on the twentieth the little Holbein Theatre was re-opening for its first Season with Hilda as its new director, backed by the great impresario, Gregor Gustave.

Lottie had always adored the Season. Usually, unless she had to go on one of Auntie's errands, she hung about the theatre, sniffing the excitement that filled it from the wardrobe room upstairs down to the dressing rooms in what used to be the cellars. Now it was all happening again: posters were going up, 'All over London,' Auntie told Lottie.

Gregor Gustave had had the theatre refurbished. 'It was shabby beyond belief,' said Hilda, but she and

Gustave had been careful to keep it exactly the same: the rose-damask walls, gilded white woodwork, seats covered in velvet, sconce lights in tiers and rose-velvet stage curtains.

On the night it would be swept and garnished; in the foyer, a great basket of red roses would be set in front of an easel holding a portrait of Madame as the Humming Bird in her brother's ballet, *Cat Among the Pigeons*. The box office telephone would soon be ringing; the seating plans filled – 'We hope,' said Hilda. Zanny, Madame's old dresser, would be vying with Auntie for attention. Emil, Zanny's husband and the theatre's handyman and commissionaire, was pressing his uniform. In the pit the music was ready – orchestra rehearsals had already begun. The conductor's rostrum was in place, the piano tuned; a harp showed a glimpse of its gilt, as if it were only waiting to be uncovered. In the dressing rooms, the costumes were being hung on their racks, tutus on their poles.

Zanny, that towering figure, went striding about, shouting orders at the dancers, while Auntie stayed quietly in control. This different Auntie only had to lift a tutu over a nervous dancer's head and say, 'Stand still, dear, while I fasten your bodice,' for the dancer to be soothed, while her, 'Remember, don't put your hands down on your waist, that'll dirty your tutu, and if you have to sit down or stand against a wall, lift it up against your back,' was always obeyed.

Hilda was giving a short ballet of her own, 'Very modern and bold, even shocking,' said the dancers but they and Gustave liked it. Balancing that was the classical *grand pas* from Paquita – recommended by Gregor Gustave because no ballet could better show the quality of its *corps de ballet* and, in compliment to Madame, he and Hilda had decided to revive *Cat Among the Pigeons* with choreography by Jan Holbein and in which Madame had made that appearance as the little Humming Bird. Now the Humming Bird was to be danced by Archie. 'Why a boy?' asked jealous Zoë. 'When Madame was a little girl?'

'I suppose it wouldn't be fair to God if I asked Him if Archie could break his leg,' Lottie said to Auntie.

It was wise of Hilda to revive *Cat Among the Pigeons* but also ambitious and she herself was dancing Innocenzia, the first pupil, a principal role. No wonder she was tired and strained. 'How she finds the time!' said Auntie but, like Madame, Hilda would always find time. She had, though, no time at all for little girls who, as it seemed to her, did not want to work and, 'If you're so tired,' she snapped at Lottie, 'you can sit down. I'll see you after class.'

'And what', asked Hilda, 'have you been doing that has made you not fit to dance just now when it's so important?'

Hilda's skin was glistening with sweat, her back and legs were aching. She also had to keep an eye on the clock; it was almost time for rehearsal and, before it, she had an appointment with the lights man, a most important person in the production but, I must be fair, thought Hilda. 'Are you feeling ill? Have you hurt yourself?' she asked and, when Lottie shook her head, 'Is there trouble at home?'

'Yes, trouble, but joy. Such joy!'

Lottie should have said that but could not find the words. Hilda only saw the pale anxious little face suddenly 'Radiant,' she told Lion afterwards. Then wariness came down. Can I tell Hilda? Lottie was wondering. Can I trust her? She had to trust her. 'You see, I have a new little puppy,' said Lottie.

Hilda saw with devastating quickness. 'A puppy! *Now!* When you and your aunt should be working every minute of the day,' and Hilda demanded, 'Who's looking after it?'

'Not it – him. I – I found him. He was lost.' That was more or less truthful. 'He's beautiful. Oh, Hilda . . .' but Lottie saw she was rhapsodising to a cold flint-hard face.

'You little idiot!' flared Hilda. 'It doesn't matter what he is, you can't look after him.'

'I can.'

'And ruin your dancing as you have these last two days?' and Hilda said what the kind lady had said, 'A puppy needs as much attention as a baby. No wonder you're tired out.'

'I'm trying to arrange things.'

'Arrange things! Listen, Lottie. Madame – I, too – we have made you as good a dancer as a child can be.' ('There is no reason', Madame often used to say, 'why, within its small compass, a child shouldn't be perfect.') 'Madame and I,' said Hilda, 'and you, too, Lottie, have been making yourself a dancer all these years. Now you have a chance, a big chance, given to few, *few* children, a chance for what we have all worked for and wanted – I can guess your auntie has prayed – and you'll let that chance go, just for a dog?'

'He's not just a dog. He's Prince.'

'Prince!' Hilda's exasperation broke. 'Has it never occurred to you', said this furious icy Hilda, 'that you are cheating your aunt? That you are letting me down? I know I don't mean much to you but I have worked and tried. Worst of all, you are betraying Madame.'

'Betraying!' Lottie looked at Hilda with horrified eyes.

'Yes, betraying. That's true, isn't it?'

Lottie shut her eyes because the classroom seemed to reel round her.

On Madame's last day – 'Only we didn't know it was

her last,' Auntie had said with tears – Madame had sent for Lottie. She had been in her big red-curtained bed, a shawl, soft and white, over her shoulders instead of the pansy jacket, a vase of her favourite red roses on the table. 'She's tired,' Zanny had warned Lottie. 'So tired she mixed me up,' Lottie told Auntie afterwards. 'Is that you, Niura?' Madame had whispered. 'Niura, always listen to the nightingale.'

Lottie did not need to ask, 'What nightingale?' Why it had made such a deep impression on her she did not know; she had never forgotten about Niura and the grandmother who taught her to make time for the nightingales but Madame had looked so far away that Lottie had put her hand on the thin withered old one. 'It's not Niura, Madame. It's me, Lottie.'

Madame had raised herself and then sank back on the pillows. 'Ah, Lottie!' Madame smiled. Then she had reached out and taken Lottie's other hand. 'I wanted to see you because ...' Madame had shut her eyes and Lottie thought she had gone to sleep, except that she still held her, Lottie's, hands. Lottie waited and Madame opened her eyes and looked at her. 'What nuisances you children have always been to me,' said Madame. 'Using me and knowing so much better than your elders.'

'Pardon?' asked Lottie.

'Never mind,' and Madame had smiled, a proud sweet

smile. 'Some nuisances are worth it, not? Never forget, Charlotte, you were born to be a dancer and that I, Anna Holbein, said it. Never forget. Promise,' and Lottie had promised but now she saw Prince running across the lawn, felt him in her arms, his warmth held close. Auntie had never been a person for hugs and kisses; when Lottie had been a baby the girls had often cuddled her but, like all dancers, they came and went. Madame had sometimes put back a lock of hair, touched Lottie's cheek; Zanny sometimes kissed her goodnight, Lottie had not asked for more, simply got on as best she could with her own life but, from the first moment she saw Prince, she had known there were no bounds to the love that a puppy, that bundle of naughtiness and sweetness, could give – and hadn't Madame said, 'Cats *and* dogs'?

'I can't help it, Hilda,' she pleaded, 'I can't.'

Cheat. Betray. Treacherous. Biting words. In her temper, tiredness and disappointment, Hilda had forgotten she was speaking to a ten-year-old child. It was too much and 'No,' Lottie had wailed aloud. 'No, Hilda. No.'

'Yes,' said Hilda and walked out of the room.

In the darkening classroom Lottie cried as she had never cried – when Madame died she had been too stunned to cry. Now the accumulation of the last three days, the dragging out of bed at six o'clock, rushing to and from school, the hungriness of having had less than half her dinner, the disgrace of her dancing seemed to have won and she was defeated.

She knew that Prince was waiting at home, by now perhaps frantic and wet, that she ought to be getting overworked Auntie's supper, but she could not move, only weep and weep, holding to the *barre*, her head down on its woodenness, while the chill and shadows of the studio seemed all round her.

'Lottie. Lottie.' It was a man's voice. The door opened, letting in a stream of light and there was Lion. 'Lottie.' Then, as his eyes took in the hopeless huddled figure, he was across the room. 'My dear, dear little girl. You mustn't cry like this.'

Lottie knew little about Lion, only that he was really Lionel Ray – Lion suited him much better – and that he was in love with Hilda, all the children knew that, But I never knew that he was nice, thought Lottie as he held her against his warmth and strength. 'There, there,' said Lion as to a baby, which, at this moment, Lottie found wonderfully comforting. 'There. You mustn't take this so much to heart. I know Hilda can be sharp – she has told me all about it and I think she's sorry. Tomorrow she'll be sorrier still.'

'It – it wasn't Hilda. It was me,' Lottie said between

sobs. 'She was right. She *is* right.' That brought a fresh burst of sobbing.

'Not always,' said Lion and, 'Lottie, did you know Madame had a little dog?'

'Madame?' Lottie was so startled that her tears dried. '*Madame?*'

'Yes. A Pomeranian called Glinka. Everyone told her not to have him but she would. He was a perfect little pest,' said Lion. 'Ask Zanny, but we all learned to put up with him.'

'You knew him?'

'Did I not?' said Lion. 'When I was your age I was always having to take him out when Zanny couldn't, or wouldn't.' Taught for nothing, like Lottie, Lion did odd jobs. 'Out in the garden, up on the Heath. Up and down the street, and now,' said Lion, 'I'm going to take you home. I want to see your Glinka.'

It was as if Lion had worked small miracles: when he delivered Lottie to Verbena Road, Auntie was home before her for once and, for once, wreathed in smiles. She had taken Prince out, given him a saucer of bread and milk and was cooking. 'Sausages!' cried Lottie. She could smell them.

'A feast,' said Lion.

'Yes. Because . . .' said Auntie, but she waited until

Lion had gone to say this, 'because, Lottie, do you know what? Hilda is paying me overtime. She says I should have had it years ago. I expect it simply didn't occur to Madame,' said loyal Auntie. 'But look, this week it's nearly double my week's pay.'

'Well, you worked quite twice that time.'

'Yes, and gladly, but now I'll be able to give you some pocket money, Lottie, and that will pay for Prince's food.' Auntie had made no comment on Lottie's tear-stained face, which meant she had heard about Hilda. 'Come, love. A cup of tea will do you good.'

A little later a knock came at the door. It was Mr Soper, who put down a large bundle of newspapers tied with string. 'People collect them to take to the church which sells them,' he said, 'but I don't see why the church should have them all.'

Later still another knock. 'Edna always rings the bell,' Auntie began to reassure Lottie but Lottie had already heard a twittering and, yes, it was Miss Dorcas and Miss Dora.

Though on Sundays, and other times too, Lottie went up to their attic, the twins had not come to the flat before which perhaps was why they twittered more than usual but now they came in and, before Auntie could ask them to sit down, 'We don't think it's right,' said Miss Dorcas.

'Not right at all,' said Miss Dora.

'Not right?' Auntie was perplexed but Lottie knew this was something to do with Prince and sure enough, '*She* said you'll have to get rid of him,' said Miss Dorcas.

'Rid of him.' Miss Dora nodded. 'She', of course, was Mrs Cuthbert.

'Your very own pet! Imagine us getting rid of Victor.'

'Or Sylvie.' Miss Dorcas and Miss Dora were puffed up with indignation.

'All the same, it's not right,' said Miss Dorcas. 'She's been watching you, Lottie. She says you run home in your school break and again at dinner time.'

'Your dinner time.'

'It's not right, dearie, to get so tired.'

'But I have to,' said Lottie.

'No,' said Miss Dorcas.

'No.' Miss Dora was actually firmer.

'If you would trust us with a key – I mean you, Miss Tew – we'll come down and let Prince out.'

'Out mid-morning.'

'Give him his little dinner at one o'clock.'

'His din-dins.'

'And take him out again. We'll be very careful.'

'Very very careful.'

'Like with the budgies.'

'Keep him on his lead.'

'Shut the garden gate.'

'Then, when he's older, take him for a ta-ta.'

Lottie was not sure what a ta-ta was but it sounded pleasant and, if a halo of blue wings, like Victor's and Sylvie's, had come to circle round those two white heads, Lottie would not have been surprised; she could have knelt down and kissed Miss Dorcas's and Miss Dora's comfortable felt slippers.

'It isn't *right* to trouble you . . . ' Auntie began.

'It is right.' Again there was this unaccustomed firmness. 'You, Miss Tew, and we, all of us who know Lottie, have to consider her dancing. That is of prime importance.'

'Prime,' said Miss Dora. Lottie had never imagined them using words like that but even with dear Miss Dorcas and Miss Dora it seemed everything, inexorably, came back to dancing.

'Well, you do seem to be getting everything your own way,' said Mrs Cuthbert.

'Yes.'

Lottie was not telling Mrs Cuthbert how filled she was with gratitude and wonder but, 'The audition's tomorrow then we shall see,' said Mrs Cuthbert with relish. 'Queen's Chase is a boarding school. What'll you do with Prince then?'

'I haven't got there yet,' said Lottie.

*

'It isn't betraying Madame.' Curled up in bed with Prince, Lottie had put, as it were, a small snug shell over them both from which everything and everyone else was shut out. 'It isn't betraying Madame.' Madame had never said a word about Her Majesty's Ballet or Queen's Chase *though* she had about cats and dogs. 'I'll go on in my ordinary day school,' Lottie was telling Madame. 'Then, when I'm grown up, I'll do what Hilda did, learn about stage lighting and scenery and costumes and music.' She was not sure about music; she had never tried to do anything with music except listen to it and count it. 'And I can't invent things so I can't be a choreographer.' A stage-manager seemed best; Auntie always said she, Lottie, was a splendid manager. 'I'll manage the Holbein Theatre for you, Madame, to the end of my days,' vowed Lottie. 'You had Glinka. You'll understand,' and as she fell almost comfortably asleep, 'I only have to be very careful not to dance too well at the audition.'

# CHAPTER IV

'Will you come in now, girls.'

Lottie had had good-luck cards from Miss Dorcas and Miss Dora – they were looking after Prince for the day; their card came through the letter box. Mr Soper pushed his under the door, and even Mrs Cuthbert sent one with, 'You can but try and do your best.'

'So kind of everyone,' said Auntie, but it was, of course, Holbein's that counted.

Yesterday, after her last coaching, Hilda had given Lottie a sprig of white heather and kissed her. 'I know you'll make us proud of you.' Lottie had had to look at the floor.

Lion had added to the embarrassment: he had laughed and said, 'No need to look so gloomy. This time tomorrow you'll be proud as punch and there'll be a big box of chocolates waiting for you,' and Zanny had told her:

'Madame always said a little prayer, a Hail Mary, before she danced, you do that too.' While, 'Remember Madame,' said Emil which was the one thing Lottie knew she must not do.

Auntie helped her off with the jersey and skirt she had worn over her leotard. 'A whole day away from Holbein's with the Season so close?' Auntie had been shocked.

'Of course you must go with Lottie,' Hilda had said. 'In any case, as her guardian you'll have to see the director.'

'Oh dear!' said Auntie.

'Probably the bursar too.'

'What's a bursar?'

'The person who looks after the money. He will show you how to apply for a grant,' and Hilda said, 'Miss Tew, you must try and realise, it costs thousands of pounds to train a child at that school.'

'Thousands of pounds for Lottie!' Auntie's eyes looked as dazzled as if someone had offered her the Crown Jewels. Then the vision faded. 'If she gets in.'

Hilda seemed to think there was not any 'if'. 'Coming from Holbein's, I should have thought they would have taken her without an audition,' she had said, 'but I suppose they felt they had to see some others. I've heard there's a little girl from Australia who is extremely talented.'

'Oh dear!' said Auntie again, and now, when she saw

the other girls, they all looked so well groomed and well fed that she fell into despair. 'Lottie, I don't think I've done well for you at all.'

'Madame thought you had,' said Lottie and could have bitten her tongue out. She must not, she dared not, think of Madame now but it seemed, as soon as she came anywhere near dancing or even thought about it, Madame was there.

Opposite Lottie and Auntie, with both her father and mother – 'So well dressed,' whispered Auntie – was an exceptionally pretty little girl. 'Now *she* is what I call a taking child!' She was more than that. Lottie recognised the poise, the way the child held herself and, She's been trained, thought Lottie. Well, so have I, and an answering poise rose in her.

The mother was lovingly twisting the girl's hair into a knot on the top of the golden head and, while she twisted, was giving anxious instructions. 'You will remember your left foot, won't you, darling, the heel well forward when you take your positions. Let your eyes follow your hand. Chin not too high . . . '

Perhaps she's the teacher, not the mother, thought Lottie.

'Irene, are you listening?' said the lady.

'No,' answered Irene.

'Darling, don't fuss her,' said the man.

Surely he would not call a teacher 'darling', thought Lottie, as he, himself, picked up a white shawl and wrapped it round this Irene's shoulders. He spoke with an accent and, 'She must be the Australian girl,' whispered Lottie.

'The one with talent. Oh dear!' said Auntie.

Immediately, 'She's not the only one,' said Lottie.

All the children with long hair had it up in a knot or plaited into a coronal like Lottie. All wore leotards and had a number cloth pinned on their chests and backs. Lottie was number five, Irene number one, which was fitting – she seemed an important little girl – but Lottie knew, and had known from her first baby class, that, in places like Her Majesty's Ballet just as it had been at Holbein's, it was not how important you were that mattered but how you danced. That Irene could dance she was sure.

Number two was a small dark-haired child with a mischievous face. 'She's got dimples,' whispered Auntie.

'That doesn't mean she can dance,' said Lottie.

Number three – tall, with fair, not golden, hair – was practising *grands battements*, just as Holbein's dancers did off-stage to warm themselves up before each performance. To Auntie the *battements* looked spectacular. 'Look at the height of that leg!'

'She jerks,' said Lottie as soon as she looked. 'The rest of her body should be still.'

There were two more girls: number four, brown-haired, blue eyes, who had, Lottie was to find, sharp elbows and a smile she seemed able to turn on and off without feeling it, while number six had copper-coloured hair and a most determined face. Well, I can be that too, thought Lottie and, as the secretary called, 'Come along now, girls,' and they filed through a door leading into an even bigger studio, Lottie could not help being on her mettle.

'What is mettle?' Long ago she had asked Madame that – it had been one of Madame's favourite words – and, 'It's what is in you,' Madame had said. 'Your inmost spirit. Ardent!' Madame's eyes had lit with memories of triumphs. 'Ardent! Strong! Show them!' Madame had cried. 'Show them your mettle. How else can they recognise you?'

Today 'they' were the Panel.

A young student teacher in regulation teacher's dress, black, flowing, with a divided skirt so that she could demonstrate steps, led the six candidates in and told them to skip in a circle round the room, 'To warm yourselves up.' To skip, in the ballet world, is not as easy as it sounds: feet must be picked up smartly, kept pointed while body and head are held erect.

As they passed the Panel's table, Lottie saw that there were four of them. It was only afterwards that she learned who they were: the small one was Miss Jean McKenzie, senior ballet mistress at Queen's Chase. The tall one, Miss Elizabeth Baxter, was principal of both junior and senior schools – she took the audition. At first she seemed frightening but when she spoke to the children her voice was kind and reassuring: 'It's all right,' she said to the small number two, who seemed almost too terrified to move. 'It doesn't matter if you make mistakes, just dance. Ah, that's better.'

Only one of the Panel was a man, young, dressed in a turtle-necked jersey and flannels. 'He's in charge of ballet at the Theatre Royal,' Auntie was to tell Lottie – Auntie had recognised him from Holbein's; Lottie only knew he had a smile that seemed to include all the anxious girls.

Most arresting of all was the lady in the centre who, even when she sat still, had a polished brilliance that filled Lottie with delighted awe. She was slim, gracefully poised, chestnut-haired and had extraordinary grey-green eyes. 'She's the ballerina, Ennis Glyn,' the girls breathed it to one another as they passed, they did not dare speak aloud, and, 'She's the director of the ballet schools.'

'The director is the head even over the principal,' the tall fair girl whispered.

Lottie's gaze kept coming back to Ennis Glyn. I would do anything, *anything*, thought Lottie, if I could please her.

'Doesn't it make you think?' Auntie said afterwards. 'All those important busy people, sparing time just to see a few children dance,' but it was not just to see them dance. One day, one of these hopefuls might, just might, hold a part of the future of Her Majesty's Ballet in her hand.

The skips had stopped. All six were panting and, 'To the *barre*, girls,' said Miss Baxter. It was for the *pliés*, deep knee bends, that opened every class.

As she went through the familiar exercises, Lottie, out of the corner of her eye, could see a girl – it was the fair number four – doing what Madame called 'tricks': a pretty little flick of the wrist, a self-conscious bringing in of her arm. 'You don't look at anybody else in class,' had been one of Madame's dicta but, Of course you do, thought Lottie, how else are you to learn? Sometimes you learn what not to do, and Lottie was even more careful of her arms and hands. The children worked at the *barre* then came into the centre. '*Port de bras*,' the young teacher told them and the pianist began a Chopin nocturne. Lottie always loved these slow movements, the arms lifted for each position, eyes and head following them. 'Gently, naturally ...' Madame used almost to croon. 'Gently. Keep your body still.'

'*Chassé arabesque* to the right.' Lottie wobbled on her first *arabesque* and felt a dark tide of disgrace creep up her neck into her face until, 'Never mind if you wobble,' came Miss Baxter's cheerful voice. 'Just see how high your leg can go,' and, next time Lottie's leg was held firmly in what even Madame would have thought a creditable *arabesque* but when she saw Irene's, Lottie's heart seemed to beat a little harder and tremors of excitement ran through her.

The audition was not all exercises: they did a jaunty little Irish jig – I did that when I was six, thought Lottie. In fact she thought the audition easy until, 'From the corner, one by one,' the young teacher told them. 'Four *galops*, starting right foot, *chassé*, *relevé* into *arabesque*, stretching arms in the third, turn' – it was almost a pirouette – 'and hold.' It was tricky. Lottie, next to last, saw the girls fail one by one until Irene, dancing just before Lottie, managed it the second time without a fault as far as Lottie could see and, as she made her own preparation, she began Madame's prayer but had only time for, 'Hail Mary ...' when, taking a deep breath, she had to start. 'Never mind if you make a mistake. Just show us how you can dance and you like it,' Miss Baxter said again and Lottie suddenly found she was dancing with her whole mind, body and strength.

'Say thank you to the pianist,' – curtsys – 'thank you to the Panel,' – more curtsys and, 'Thank you,' said Miss

Baxter. 'Now run back into the studio you came from. Don't take off your things till you're told. Wait.'

'Wait!'

The room was filled with tension as anxious grown-ups bundled the girls up in coats and jerseys and wiped the sweat off faces, necks and hands. Nobody spoke: all of them sat watching the door and trying to guess what was going on behind it. Lottie had seen the papers on the Panel's table, she had even caught a glimpse of her own photograph pinned to one of them. She had seen pencils marking them. Hilda had told her they were not marks, like school marks, but assessments 'of every part of you,' said Hilda, 'head to foot – your extension, your turn out, elevation.'

What none of them knew was that almost immediately the director had crossed out two names: Sharp Elbows and Copper Head. Though the two went through all the movements the Panel did not look at them again.

Tension grew: only number four was still smiling. Suddenly, number two, the small dark girl, burst into tears. 'Take me home,' she wailed. 'I want to go home. I know I didn't do it properly. I know.'

'Hush darling. You don't *know*,' her mother tried to soothe her. 'It will be just a few minutes longer.'

The crying only grew more frantic, and the helpless mother had to take her out.

That unnerved all the others. The fair girl fidgeted with her fingers, her feet beat a maddening tattoo on the floor until her father put out a hand. Copper Head stared at the floor while Lottie felt confidence ebbing out of her very toes.

'Who trained you?' Copper Head had asked after she had seen Lottie's *arabesque*.

'Madame Holbein.'

'Never heard of her,' said Copper Head.

That had shaken Lottie. Was Madame, then, not as famous as the world of Holbein thought? Could it be possible that Hilda, Lion, Auntie, Zanny, all of them had been mistaken and that she, Lottie, had been taught wrongly?

'You little half-wit,' Hilda was to say when Lottie told her. 'Because one ignorant little girl ...' but for the moment Lottie felt sick. She glanced across the room at Irene. Irene smiled at her, but was there, could there be, such a difference in their dancing?

'Auntie, I'm going to throw up,' Lottie had almost whispered it when the door opened and half dreading, half hopeful, expectancy ran through the room.

'Numbers two, three, four and six can go now. The Panel are sorry but they do not think you could really cope with Her Majesty's Ballet School.'

There was a sound like a sigh, a deep breath let out.

The fair girl gasped; the smile was wiped off number four's face – and off her mother's; their cheeks grew red. Copper Head looked stunned but the secretary went steadily on. 'Number one and number five, the Panel would like to see you again, please.'

So poor little number two was right, thought Lottie. She was glad Sharp Elbows was out; she had not liked the fair girl either, nor her dancing, but she was sorry for Copper Head who had tried so hard. Now it was between Irene and herself: two girls, one place.

Not one of the little girls, not even number three, had thought of the audition as a competition in which the best dancer would win. 'Sometimes out of twenty children we don't take even one,' said Miss Baxter. Each danced as well as she could, but for herself, and now, though Irene and Lottie smiled at one another, as soon as they came back into the audition room, they forgot everything except dancing.

'Begin, as you did before with a few skips to warm you up,' said Miss Baxter, 'then show us that *enchaînement*, four *galops*, starting right foot, *chassé* ...' Irene and Lottie looked at one another. It would be that one! But their eyes shone with excitement. It was not the stretch that was so difficult but the control needed for the slow *chassé* after the *galops*, more control for the turn, when they had to remember head, eyes, arms; still more when, coming out of it, they had to 'hold', head up, body still, foot pointed.

Neither of them made a mistake. 'The last part was the worst,' Lottie told Hilda afterwards. 'We had to take off our shoes and the teacher took us to the *barre*.' Under the scrutiny of those four pairs of expert eyes, the teacher tried the girls' legs, stretching them to see how high they could go, how far they could turn out. 'Ouch! That hurt!' Lottie wanted to cry. 'Then we had to come into the centre and lie down on the floor, flat to the ground, draw our feet up together – we looked like frogs – to see how far our knees would go to the ground. We had to get up and stand again but this time, just stand, head up, legs straight. I kept thinking about my knobbly knees – Irene's were perfect – while the Panel looked and looked and looked. It went on for ever!'

Then, 'Thank you,' said Miss Baxter. 'You can take your shoes and go.' No more than that, not the least flicker of a sign.

As they went through the doorway, Irene and Lottie stayed close together as Lottie whispered, 'If it's me, I'll be almost sorry it isn't you.'

'Me too,' Irene whispered back.

'You can get dressed now, girls. Then please wait,' the secretary said again and disappeared through the door.

Time seemed to go on and on. Even Irene was hushed; her mother had tried to hold her hand but Irene pulled away and went to sit by her father, who put his arm round her. Lottie sat silently by Auntie, who had her hands clenched in her cotton gloves. They could hear the studio clock ticking on and on.

At last the secretary came back and she was laughing. *Laughing* now! All of them glared at her with indignation until she said, 'Congratulations, girls. I'm happy to tell you, Irene and Charlotte, that the Panel have decided to accept you both.'

# CHAPTER V

'Charlotte, you don't look very glad,' said Ennis Glyn in the director's office. 'Is there anything wrong?'

The secretary had told them they were making an extra place at Queen's Chase – 'Even if we put a bed on the ceiling we would never let a promising dancer go,' Miss Baxter explained afterwards – and now, 'Will you take an hour and go and have some lunch,' said the secretary. 'Come back, please, at half past one. Irene and Charlotte have to see the doctor and then you must both meet the director and the principal.' She said again, 'Congratulations, girls.'

Irene had been so rapturous that she was almost dancing again but Lottie stayed so stiff and still that Irene's mother asked, 'Don't you feel well, dear?'

'It's the shock,' said Auntie. She did not know of the deeper shock; Lottie's carefully thought-out plan lay shattered. She had danced too well, so well that for three hours she had never once thought of Prince.

'It's just that she's shy,' Auntie was saying now. She had difficulty in not calling Miss Glyn 'my lady': in her time Auntie had seen many lords and ladies, as she often told Mrs Cuthbert, 'Dukes and duchesses too, and a princess – only from behind the curtain, as it were, but I know what's what.' Ennis Glyn was not only the director of the schools and a famous ballerina, she was a lady and a gracious one; now she was looking so thoughtfully at Lottie that Auntie quaked. Was Lottie going to spoil it all?

Only two hours ago, Lottie had felt she would move heaven and earth to please Ennis Glyn; now she dreaded her and the terrible part was that she could not explain, dared not explain, only look dumbly at this new-found goddess.

'She's shy,' repeated Auntie, 'and doesn't show her feelings.'

Show my feelings! If Lottie had done that, Miss Glyn's office, furnished not like an office but a beautiful drawing room, would have gone up in smoke. Lottie squeezed her hands between her knees as she gathered her courage. Then, 'Please,' she said, 'do I have to be a boarder?'

'Well, you can't travel from Hampstead to Buckingham Park and back every day, can you?'

'N-no.' The net was closing round her.

'You may be homesick at first, Charlotte,' Ennis Glyn said gently, 'but all of us dancers have to make sacrifices.' She could not know that, in this case, the sacrifice was a confident trusting little dog whose world was Lottie. Ennis Glyn saw her eyes blaze with indignation and, 'You do want to dance, Charlotte?' she asked.

'Of course.' There was no argument about that, particularly after meeting Irene. '*Of course*,' at which Ennis Glyn gave her a warm smile, 'I think you will love being at Queen's Chase.'

'I'll have to, won't I?' That was an answer that made Ennis Glyn look at Lottie again.

The long day was not over yet. While Auntie saw the bursar, Lottie had to wait in the hall.

It was an impressively high hall; domed, with a long staircase leading up from it and, on every side, big mahogany doors discreetly closed. Lottie had been through two of them, to Miss Glyn's drawing-room office and Miss Baxter's. Behind two others came the sound of voices and typewriters, of telephones ringing, the secretaries at work. A traffic of people came through the hall: young dancers – they looked grown-up to Lottie – in every kind of bizarre clothes, leg warmers, jerseys, smocks, tunics, scarves, all carrying bags bulging, particularly with shoes. Pianists came and went, their music cases bulging too. There were pupil teachers in black and older men and women, some in wonderful clothes, some in jerseys and slacks who, Lottie thought, must be teachers. The whole building was a hive, not of bees, but of dancers, more than she had ever seen or imagined and all – even if they stopped and talked or even chattered – were purposeful. Sitting on a small wooden chair Lottie watched till her eyes ached. She ached to go home. How long, wondered Lottie, how much longer, was Auntie going to be?

There was a pause in the flow: afternoon classes must have settled down, thought accustomed Lottie. In the empty hall there were only the typewriter sounds, a murmur of voices behind the closed doors and her small self sitting half asleep on that hard chair.

Suddenly she was wide awake. With a loud slithering noise a boy came sliding down the banisters. Slide down the banisters – *here!* she thought, shocked into alertness. The slide ended in a resounding 'whop' as the boy hit the newel post and bounced off on to the floor. 'Bounced' was the right word. In a second he was up again, rubbing his bottom with such a rueful though laughing face that Lottie almost laughed too, but she did not like boys. 'You shouldn't do that here,' she said, as prim as Auntie.

'It's just here I want to do it,' he said. Still rubbing, he came over to where she was sitting. He was not a usual boy: he had silken black hair worn longer than most boys, black eyes alert with curiosity and mischief, and a smooth olive skin, through which the red showed. His lips were too red for a boy and his teeth were ... pretty? thought Lottie. Pretty was a word for a girl, but they were pretty, small, even and dazzlingly white. She was also struck by the elegance of his clothes: black velvet corduroy trousers, a red jersey that looked as if it were made of silk, red socks, polished black shoes.

He isn't English, thought Lottie, though he spoke as if he were. 'It was just for fun,' he said and, as Lottie would not allow her expression to change he asked, 'Don't you ever have fun?'

She could not answer that: she did not really know what fun was and he went on. 'I needed it. I've been auditioning all morning.'

'So have I,' said Lottie. 'I didn't see you.'

'Because you were with the girls.'

The way he said 'girls' nettled her.

'Girls are as good as boys.'

'Not here, they're not. In dancing it's the boys who count.'

'It isn't. It's the girls.'

'For every boy, there are five hundred girls.'

There was some truth in that. 'Five, perhaps,' said exact Lottie, 'five hundred, never.'

It seemed he could not keep still, swinging himself around the table and on the newel post, but there was nothing in the hall to interest him and he came back to her. 'Why are you waiting here?'

'My aunt is with the bursar.'

'I bet you don't know what a bursar is.'

'I do. He's the gentleman who shows you how to get the grant.'

'Grant? You mean money. For what?'

'To pay for me.'

To her that seemed a matter of course but, 'My papa doesn't need to see the bursar for *that*,' said the boy in contempt. 'He's rich. He's got more than a hundred cars.'

'Liar.'

''Tisn't a lie. He has a car-hire business, see?' and he said in glee, 'You never thought of that, did you?'

Lottie not only had not thought of it, she had not heard of cars for hire.

'If your papa's so wonderful, I'm surprised you are waiting here,' said Lottie. 'Or perhaps it's your mother.'

'No mother, thank you.' She saw that the mischief was gone from his eyes, his face was hard. '*Thank you.*' He ran up the stairs, she heard him whistling as again he came sliding down. This time he remembered the newel post, swung himself off, came back to her and bragged, 'I was the only one who passed out of seven boys and d'you know why?' She did not want to know but he went on, 'Because I'm a brilliant dancer, that's why.'

'But you mustn't say so.' Lottie was shocked at this boasting.

'Look,' and on the marble floor he turned two quick cartwheels, light as a sprite. 'Could you do that?'

'If I wanted to,' but she was not sure she could, not in the same way. She could see why he had passed.

'You've passed too?'

'Yes,' and at last such despair welled up in Lottie over Prince that she wanted to cry and she turned her face away; then she felt a hand on her shoulder, a small strong hand.

A voice, so soft and charming that she could not believe it was his, said, 'Don't be upset. I didn't mean to upset you,' but she had not forgiven him about the girls and shook him off.

'I'm not upset!'

That challenged him. 'I'm surprised you passed. You're so skinny. There was one pretty girl,' he said. 'Lovely gold hair.'

'That's Irene, my friend.' Lottie still saw Irene in a haze, and Irene's mother – she was pretty too – had said, 'Your aunt told me you were trained by Anna Holbein herself. You lucky lucky girl.'

Remembering that, Lottie held her head high as she asked, 'Where were you trained?'

'I wasn't. I never have been.'

'*Never?*' She couldn't believe it. 'Then why are you here?'

'Because I wanted to dance and go in at the top. This is the top. My papa found that out.'

'Never been trained yet you passed?' She was mystified.

'Ennis Glyn said training didn't matter.'

Didn't matter! All those years! What Ennis Glyn had said was, 'Even if a child hasn't been trained – it's so difficult to undo bad habits ...' 'Like the fair girl's tricks,' Lottie would have said but the boy was going on.

'Also, more than anything in the world I want to dance.' He was deeply serious. Then, quick as a flash, he darted back upstairs and slid down the banisters yet again. Ennis Glyn's door opened and a gentleman came out just in time to see him.

He was plump, dressed in a pale grey suit and Lottie saw a great deal of gold about him, gold watch chain across his waistcoat, gold cuff-links, a gold ring. He was dark-haired like the boy, creamy-skinned, but his eyes, she saw, were brown and looked anxious as he heard the noise. The boy hit the newel post and bounced off. The gentleman, quick and light on his feet as many plump people are, was across the floor, seized the boy and gave him a resounding smack across the bottom. 'Oh, no!' Lottie wanted to cry, she had not seen a child hit before – while a torrent of words poured out. 'Disgraziato! Cretino! You shall not come here if you cannot behave. You come along home, this instant! Disgraziato!' and the boy was led away by the ear.

He was soon back. 'I didn't say goodbye to you.' And to Lottie's disgust he kissed her twice, once on each cheek.

'Go *away*,' but he had gone.

It seemed quiet without him; then Lottie looked down and froze.

Close to her foot, on the floor was an enormous spider, bigger than any she had seen or imagined with black hairy legs, bulging wicked black eyes that were looking at her. Hastily she drew up her legs on to the chair but her foot must have touched it because it moved. Lottie's scream was so piercing that it rang through the hall as did another and another.

All the doors opened, first of all Miss Baxter's; she and Auntie came out. 'Careful!' shrieked Lottie. 'Look! Look!'

Everyone looked. She heard Auntie's gasp. Another gasp went round, then, 'All right,' called Miss Baxter. 'Charlotte, stay on your chair. Don't move anybody. Linda,' she called to her secretary, 'bring me the heavy shovel and a wastepaper basket.'

Slowly, step by step, Miss Baxter advanced with the shovel, Linda behind her with the wastepaper basket. The spider did not move. Miss Baxter stopped, bent down, looked and suddenly picked it up. Another gasp went round. Holding it by one of its legs so that it dangled she stood up. 'Somebody,' said Miss Baxter, 'has been visiting a joke shop.'

'Well, it might have been real,' Auntie argued afterwards. 'Big spiders do come over in cargo ships. Those joke shops are so clever. Even Miss Baxter was taken in at first.'

'It was a cruel joke,' said Miss Baxter. 'Poor Charlotte,' but Lottie was scalded with shame and fury. 'You should have guessed,' she told herself. 'Didn't Archie bring those horrible, squiggly snakes to Holbein's? I should have known.' She still, though, shuddered when she thought of the spider. 'Even if I had known, I wouldn't have touched it. And that terrible boy is coming to Queen's Chase.'

Auntie babbled all the way home: of Ennis Glyn and her graciousness; of how Miss Baxter had talked to her of Lottie's dancing – 'I was proud of you, dearie.' About the kindness of the bursar and, 'Well, you always were a quiet one,' she said as they walked up the hill from the underground station, 'but I shouldn't have thought you would be as quiet as this.'

Miss Dorcas's and Miss Dora's expectant heads appeared over the banisters – they had heard the key turn in the door. Mr Soper, too, was in his doorway, his braces hanging down over the back of his trousers which showed he had come out in a hurry. Mrs Cuthbert was not long after. 'They must all have been watching, the dear people!' cried Auntie, but Lottie had rushed into the garden with Prince and flung herself down on the grass.

'Well, she might have had the manners,' said Mrs Cuthbert, 'when we're all so interested, to come and tell us about it.'

'She should have,' Auntie had to admit. 'I don't know what's come over Lottie.'

'I do,' said Mrs Cuthbert. 'It's that little dog,' and Auntie remembered.

'Ouch!' she cried as if in pain.

'Yes,' said Mrs Cuthbert. 'You haven't much time, Amy. Today's Friday. You say you have to take Lottie to see over Queen's Chase on Monday. Term begins on Thursday so, if you don't sell him, what else?'

Auntie obviously could not think what else, and tears stung Lottie's eyes again; she had wept helplessly in the garden, and, rather than let Mrs Cuthbert see her face, had retreated into her bedroom where she stood at the window, Prince held tight in her arms.

Prince, though, wriggled to get down and next moment

was playing hide and seek all over the room: 'You can't catch me.' He showed it as plainly as if he had said it – he always did this in their games of hide and seek, his head cocked sideways until he ran, chestnut ears flying, tail wagging, to hide under the bed again.

On Saturday afternoon Lottie took refuge up on the Heath with Prince and there she met Violetta and Sam.

Sam beaming, helped Violetta out of the car but what was this? Gone were the tailored coat, the white tights and boots that were Serafina's pride. Violetta was wearing jeans, a red anorak and her hair was tied back in a pony tail. 'I wanted to look just like you,' she told Lottie.

'Like any ordinary girl!' Sam was pleased.

Lottie had not the heart to tell him that now she herself was not quite an ordinary girl.


'Dearie,' said Auntie at breakfast on Sunday, 'we'll have to try and find Prince a good home.'

'No.'

'We can put a notice in the post office: "Wanted, a kind home for a pedigree Cavalier King Charles spaniel puppy".'

'How do we know they'll be kind?'

'We'll ask for references.'

'No.'

'Lottie, we must.'

'No.'

'All right. We won't talk about it now.' Auntie, too, was glad to push it away. 'We'll wait.'

Wait for what? Neither of them knew and, that evening, when Lottie was in bed and getting drowsy, she heard Mrs Cuthbert come in.

'Where is she?' whispered Mrs Cuthbert.

'In bed and, I hope, asleep. It's Queen's Chase tomorrow, Edna, and I just don't know what to do.'

'That's exactly what I've come about. Amy, better not think about the little dog any more.'

'What do you mean, Edna?'

'For the moment, go along with it as if you were going to keep him.'

'But I can't. I wish I could but I can't.'

'I know that but . . .'

'Hush, Edna. Lottie may still be awake,' and Mrs Cuthbert sank her voice so that Lottie had to strain her ears to hear. 'Wait till she's gone,' whispered Mrs Cuthbert, 'and then . . .'

Mrs Cuthbert whispered but Lottie had heard.

# CHAPTER VI

Monday was a cool clear day as Lottie and Auntie came to Queen's Chase.

Before they joined the school, all Queen's Chase children had to see over it and meet Mrs Challoner, its headmistress and her staff. 'I don't see how I can take the time off,' Auntie had said but she had to. 'I'm your guardian,' she told Lottie.

'Guardian?' asked Lottie and then, 'I suppose I'm what they call a one-parent child.'

'Not even that,' said Auntie.

Lottie and Auntie had to take the underground train from Hampstead to Buckingham Park station, a long way – 'Right across the city, north to south,' said Auntie – then a bus to the Park itself. Put down at one of its great gates, they walked through groves of trees and open glades where herds were grazing. Herds of what? What were they? Town-bred Lottie stopped. 'They're ... Auntie, they *are*! They're deer.'

They were: red deer, smaller russet-coloured, white-spotted ones and a few big antlered stags. 'All loose!' said Lottie.

'Oh dear! I hope they're safe. They look dangerous to me.'

'They can't be dangerous or they wouldn't be loose,' but Lottie put herself between the deer and Auntie. 'Look, there are other people here.' People riding, children playing, people walking their dogs – Lottie averted her eyes from those.

'Lots of people.' Auntie was relieved and, 'I'm sure not one of them', said proud Auntie, 'is going to Queen's Chase.'


'I never dreamed!' breathed Auntie. 'Lottie, I never dreamed!'

They had walked up a drive with a notice: 'Queen's Chase. Her Majesty's Ballet Junior School' and stood gazing at the big cream stuccoed and porticoed house, with pavilions either side and roses and wide-leaved trees growing close to its walls.

'I think they must be magnolias. Lovely in the spring,' Auntie whispered. 'It's like a little palace.'

Auntie was right. Princes and princesses had lived

at Queen's Chase, dukes and duchesses. It was King Charles I who had enclosed Buckingham Park as his royal deer park; George I had built Queen's Chase as a hunting lodge. Queen Mary, the Queen's grandmother, had been born here and, as a little girl, had climbed the great cedar tree that stood in the gardens stretching behind the house.

'And to think, Lottie,' said Auntie as she dared to ring the bell at the heavy doors inside the portico, 'to think that soon you'll be part of all this!'

'Charlotte and Miss Tew?' A young woman had come to the door. 'Good afternoon. I am Daphne Layton, Mrs Challoner's secretary. Do come in.'

'So nice and friendly,' whispered Auntie and found the courage to say a fluttering, 'Thank you.'

Lottie said nothing at all. She had promised herself not to be interested in anything, not even look, but found she could not help giving glances. She caught a glimpse, to the left, of what seemed to be a museum. 'It used to be the orangery,' explained Miss Layton, but now there were photographs and posters, glass cases of shoes, fans and wigs and a statue of a dancer in a tutu which was intriguingly made of metal. The hall itself was high with a wide blue carpeted staircase, leading up from a squared marble floor.

'I'll tell Mrs Challoner you're here,' said Miss Layton.

'Will you go into her study,' but Auntie could not help lingering. The hall was dominated by a painting of a girl in a wide white dress, its flounces painted with cherries.

'Karsavina as Columbine in *Carnival*,' whispered Auntie – it seemed she had to whisper. 'She was a very great ballerina.'

'Not greater than Madame,' Lottie said instantly.

'There are two odd waifs waiting for you,' Daphne told Mrs Challoner. 'A small thin Charlotte and such a helpless-looking little aunt.'

'She can't be all that helpless to have been Anna Holbein's wardrobe mistress for more than twenty years.' Mrs Challoner was always practical. 'She's probably tough as old boots and a child can hardly be a waif if she can get herself into Queen's Chase.'

'You'll see,' said Daphne and it was true that when Mrs Challoner opened the study door, Auntie and Lottie started up, then seemed to freeze. Like a couple of startled hares, thought Mrs Challoner.

Few people, though, could remain frozen for long with Mrs Challoner: she was tall, and handsome, thought Auntie and handsomely dressed, yet she had such an immediate warmth and naturalness and was so refreshingly down to earth that Auntie was soon talking easily, even laughing, back in the joy, the excitement and achievement that this visit to Queen's Chase meant.

But only the aunt, thought Mrs Challoner. Why?

She showed them round herself; usually it was left to the girl's housemistress or the boy's housemaster. 'Well, I had just had an extremely spoiled little girl, Irene St Charles, with doting parents,' she told Daphne. 'I suppose it was the contrast.'

Lottie had followed her and Auntie like an obedient but silent shadow. 'Isn't that lovely, Lottie?' No answer. 'Lottie, look at that!' No look. Yet, as Mrs Challoner's quick eye saw, Lottie could not help giving surreptitious glances. If those glances were let loose, thought Mrs Challoner, they would be filled with all the excitement and curiosity of any child privileged to come to Queen's Chase.


Though so gracious, and seemingly so spacious, Queen's Chase was a strange house for a boarding school, 'As it was given to us we must make do,' said Mrs Challoner.

'Make do!' cried Auntie. 'This enchanting house!' but then Auntie had never seen a boarding school.

Most schools, besides their schoolrooms with desks and blackboards, art rooms, laboratories, gymnasiums, do not have in addition, three large dancing studios with *barres* along the walls and long wide mirrors. Even the Salon, the great drawing room of the house, had been made into a dance studio. 'Which ruined it,' said Mrs Challoner; the oak parquet floor had been overlaid with a sprung floor – oak is too hard on a dancer's feet; *barres* had had to be fixed to the panelling.

'A pity but we need every bit of space.' The beautiful small Yellow Drawing Room had become Mrs Challoner's study with an outer office, 'Where the secretaries work.' The Queen's Pavilion – Auntie repeated those magical words to herself, 'Queen's Pavilion' – had been made into a separate wing for the boys. 'We have forty boys.' On the other side of the house was a new block of schoolrooms but the old cobbled yard was still there, its coach house and stables made into more schoolrooms and music practice rooms. Lottie had never seen so many pianos. 'There are some in the dormitories as well,' said Mrs Challoner. 'You'll see.'

The two wings were linked, on the first floor, by two long half-circle corridors; in the upper one, the younger girls slept, 'A most peculiar dormitory but it used to be the picture gallery,' explained Mrs Challoner. Now it held an array of small white beds, each with a locker beside it. 'I expect this will be yours, Charlotte. The new girls always sleep closest to the housemistress.'

'How kind,' said Auntie. Lottie turned her back.

For all her resolutions though, interest could not help breaking through when Mrs Challoner took them down to the basement with its storerooms, changing rooms, kitchens, and a big dining hall with small red-topped tables.

'The children collect their trays and choose what they like from the canteen counter.' The first supper menu was already chalked on a blackboard ready for Thursday.

HOT HAM WITH PINEAPPLE
MASHED POTATOES
SWEETCORN
SLICED BEANS
SALADS
FRUIT TART AND CUSTARD

and, 'O-oh!' Lottie could not help that coming out. '*O-oh!*'

'Yes. We feed you six times a day,' said Mrs Challoner. 'Breakfast, and if you don't eat two courses, Charlotte, you won't be allowed to dance that day. At eleven, milk or orange juice and biscuits. Lunch at one when, again, you choose from the blackboard. Tea, same as elevenses. Supper . . . and a hot drink at bed-time.'

'*Every day?*' asked Lottie faintly.

'Every day.'

Auntie and Lottie looked at one another speechless.

Mrs Challoner showed them the schoolrooms. 'Have you done any science, Charlotte?' she asked.

'No.'

'Art? Do you like art?'

'No.'

'Will she learn French?' To Auntie, French was the peak of learning; she had never ceased to be amazed at the way Madame used to slip from English into French, French into Russian.

'Of course she will. After all, French is the language of ballet, just like Latin for medicine and botany. Have you done any nature study, Charlotte?'

'No,' but as they came back to the house through the garden, they passed an inner garden hedged with yews, the Four Yews garden, and a lily pond.

'Water lilies still in flower,' marvelled Auntie.

Beside it, Lottie saw a long low shed with a wire-netted enclosure. 'That,' said Mrs Challoner, 'is where the children keep their pets.'

'Pets!' She saw a Charlotte transformed, her face alive with interest, her eyes wide. 'You mean even *boarders* can have pets?'

'Lots of them have. All kinds of pets – rabbits, hamsters, mice. We even had a parrot and a grass snake,' and 'Do you love animals so much, Charlotte?' asked Mrs Challoner.

'Not those kind of animals.' The interest had faded.

At last they were back in the Yellow Drawing Room

where practical things had to be discussed. Auntie had been worrying about Lottie's uniform which, it had to be admitted, was unusual for a school uniform. 'Track suit?' she asked mystified. 'Does she have to have that?'

'She'll need it to put over her leotard before and after dancing – it's quite a long way to some of the studios,' said Mrs Challoner, 'but you can get one very reasonably from the wardrobe.'

'Wardrobe? You have a wardrobe *here*?'

'Indeed yes, in constant use. Would you like to see it?'

'Oh, please. *Please.*'

'Our wardrobe mistress isn't back yet but Daphne will show you the wardrobe room. Charlotte?'

Lottie shook her head but no sooner had Auntie and Daphne gone than Mrs Challoner found Lottie at her elbow, a changed Lottie, quivering with eagerness.

'Mrs Challoner, could I . . . could I ask you something? Quickly, before Auntie gets back?'

'You can ask me anything,' said Mrs Challoner, 'though I don't know if I'll be able to answer,' but something in her clear, brown and exceedingly intelligent eyes, the way she had listened to Auntie, thought Lottie – made Lottie feel she really could ask, and she stood in front of Mrs Challoner, tense from head to foot.

'You said the children here can have pets?'

'Yes.'

'Could I?'

'Of course. You'll be the same as the others,' and Lottie drew a deep breath.

'Mrs Challoner, could I – could I have a dog?'

# CHAPTER VII

'A dog?' said Mrs Challoner. 'I'm afraid that's against the rules, but tell me ... ' She listened to Lottie's story as she had listened to Auntie and only now and again saying, 'Go on,' or, 'Yes, and then?' so that Lottie, who was so bad at finding words told Mrs Challoner things she had not told before but not about the big boy snatching Prince from the pet shop – I'd better not tell anyone about that ever – but how ... She had rescued Prince and brought him home; about Mr Soper, Miss Dorcas and Miss Dora, Holbein's, Hilda, Zanny and Madame – for Mrs Challoner it cast a new light on Madame – then Glinka and,

'Could I,' asked Lottie, 'could I bring this little dog, please, Mrs Challoner? He is only a very little dog.'

Mrs Challoner did not answer at once. Then, 'If I break a rule for one person, Charlotte,' she said, 'I have to break it for all. This term there will be a hundred and twenty-six children at Queen's Chase. Suppose they all wanted to bring their dogs? At a pinch we could have a hundred and twenty-six rabbits, but not a hundred and twenty-six dogs.'

'Then – I can't have mine.'

'They have to leave theirs, Charlotte.'

'Probably they have someone to leave them with,' said Lottie.

'Auntie, couldn't you?' she had entreated.

'I wish I could,' said Auntie. 'He'd be such company but, dearie, you know that often I don't go straight to Holbein's from here. I shan't have you now to match patterns and go to the bead shop for me. I can't take a dog with me there, can I? I can't take him to Holbein's, Zanny would never let me. And sometimes I'm late home,' Auntie had said. 'Think of him all alone. I couldn't bear it.'

Lottie could not bear it either.

Miss Dorcas and Miss Dora? They had kept Prince on the day of the audition and when Lottie and Auntie went to Queen's Chase, but every day? They could not go up and down stairs all day long; if they took Prince upstairs how could the budgerigars have their flying and, also, the twins liked to go out shopping in the West End, or to the cinema. No, I can't ask Miss Dorcas and Miss Dora, decided Lottie. Mr Soper? Even partisan Lottie could see that he would not do. Hilda? Hilda would refuse. 'You can't have a dog and dancing.' Lion? But Lottie knew that, for all Lion's charm, he was not to be trusted. 'Of course I'll have Prince,' but next time Lion had to dance in Manchester, Bristol, Brussels, Paris, he would forget him. Lottie had dreadful visions of Prince left in Lion's flat, having eaten all the food, drunk all his water, if Lion remembered to give him water, and she shuddered.

There's no one. No one, Lottie thought in despair. She would not look at Mrs Challoner because she was afraid she was going to cry. Instead she looked over to the gardens of this enchanted place then said what was the most dreadful of all, 'You see I heard Auntie and Mrs Cuthbert talking – they thought I was asleep – and Mrs Cuthbert said ...' Lottie's voice shook and her hands were clenched.

'Tell me what she said,' said Mrs Challoner.

'She said, "Wait till Lottie's gone. She'll be so taken up with Queen's Chase, she'll forget about Prince. When she comes back for half-term or the weekend, tell her you've found him a good home but, actually, when she's out of the way, take him to the vet, Amy, and have him put to sleep. It'll be kindest for everyone in the end." *Kindest!* A puppy doesn't *want* to go to sleep. He's only just begun,' cried Lottie and, though she clenched her hands so hard that the nails dug into her palms, two tears rolled down her cheeks.

'Surely your aunt would never do a thing like that?'

'Mrs Cuthbert can make Auntie do what she wouldn't do – 'specially if I'm not there.'

'She ought to be boiled in oil!' said Mrs Challoner.

That, though Lottie did not know the words, was so exactly what she had been thinking all night, that the tears stopped running. A grown-up to say that! She stared at Mrs Challoner in surprised delight and, 'You do see,' whispered Lottie.

'Indeed I do see.' Mrs Challoner did not offer Lottie any useless sympathy, but lent her a handkerchief of which Lottie was in need, and she said, 'I think you must come here, Charlotte. It isn't your decision, it has been decided for you – not by anybody else but by your dancing. We won't let Prince be put to sleep, I promise you. Your aunt is right, though. We shall have to find him a good home with someone who will take him and love him.'

'I don't know anyone.' Lottie's anguish burst out. 'I can't. I can't.'

Again Mrs Challoner did not offer any sympathy. Instead she said, as if by inspiration, 'Charlotte, from what you have told me you have always followed Madame Holbein. Did Madame have Glinka for always? Ask her dresser Zanny.'

*

'Zanny, what happened to Glinka?' Lottie asked it with confidence: had not Madame said when they talked of Niura's nightingale that we need things? thought Lottie. She had even said, 'Cats, dogs ...' and, 'Zanny, what happened to Glinka?'

'Glinka? Oh, the little dog? Madame had to go on a world tour so, thank goodness, she gave him away.'

Lottie's heart sank like a stone; her last prop was taken away, particularly when Zanny went on, 'She had to, Lottie, all those foreign countries and the quarantines, besides she was to be away a year. Glinka would have forgotten her.'

That was another desolation for Lottie. Would Prince forget her? She could not bear it. 'He wouldn't. He wouldn't,' she cried out and, 'No one cares about animals at all.'

'Don't be silly.' Zanny sounded cross. 'Madame cried and cried, and she took such pains, tried everyone she knew before she decided who should have him.'

'I don't know anyone.' Lottie stopped. She did know someone.


'Vivi, today could I come to tea with you?'

Lottie had made her plan carefully. First of all she had to check Violetta's house to see if it was suitable for Prince and on Tuesday – the days were ticking away – she

93

took him up on the Heath praying that Violetta and Sam would be there. She was lucky.

'Tea with *me*!' Violetta said in delight. 'Sam, Lottie and Prince are coming to tea. Let's go now.'

'When you have had your walk,' said Sam and, to Lottie, 'Are you sure it's all right?'

'I've asked my aunt.'

'Good,' said Sam. 'Afterwards I'll run you home. Come along, little mister,' he said to Prince. 'Take Vivi for a walk.'

Violetta's home in Soho was not far from the bead shop though Lottie had never ventured into Soho's labyrinth of narrow streets. It seemed film companies had their offices there with garish posters in the windows; there were cabarets, games alleys, and night clubs. They passed restaurant after restaurant and food shops selling, to Lottie, queer food, Italian, French, Indian, Chinese, Japanese, while the pavements were crowded with people, black, white, brown, yellow, several of them jabbering so hard that they stepped into the road and Sam had to drive at a snail's pace.

He drew up at a tall house with a shop on the ground floor; the shop was called Ruffino's and the street was Webster Street – Lottie noted that carefully. The front door of the double flat upstairs was at the side. Lottie carried Prince as Sam helped Violetta up the stairs,

Violetta calling, 'Serafina! Serafina! Fai presto viene qui! Lottie and Prince have come to tea with me. Viene qui!'

The double flat was unexpectedly spacious, to Lottie's relief, with plenty of space for a small dog to play. The thick carpets, though, were fitted. I shall have to teach them about newspapers. She saw velvet curtains, chairs that had gilded edges but Violetta hurried her into her schoolroom. 'We'd like her to go to school but she won't,' said Sam. 'So she has a governess.' Then she'll be with Prince all day, thought Lottie. He wouldn't have to be alone, and her heart lifted.

She had never imagined a room like that schoolroom; even Madame's sitting room seemed cluttered and shabby beside it. It was a fairy-tale room. The wallpaper was patterned with rosebuds, there were white curtains, white rugs on the floor, pale blue furniture, even a small pale blue piano; nor could she have imagined so many toys and books. The bedroom matched it, as Lottie saw when Serafina took her to wash her hands, yet Violetta was not altogether spoiled; she was sweet and there was something wistful about her, but she was happy now, bubbling over with happiness.

A newspaper was duly spread for Prince – Serafina as well as Violetta laughed when Prince obliged. 'Che bravo cane!' cried Serafina.

The tea was sumptuous: it was not exactly tea, they

drank hot chocolate. Serafina made toast, there were nutty biscuits and Lottie had not known such cream cakes. Prince had a saucer of milk and a sponge finger. 'But you mustn't let him get fat.' Lottie almost said it.

Sam drove her home. 'You've made a lot of difference to Vivi,' said Sam and, 'Prince is the right name for you,' he told the sleepy puppy as he opened the car door for Lottie at the gate of number 5 Verbena Road. 'Come whenever you can.'

Today was Tuesday; there was just Wednesday, then . . . 'I won't be able to come for a long time,' said Lottie but Sam had driven away.

It was the last night. 'I asked Edna not to come in,' said Auntie. 'I thought we'd rather be on our own.'

Lottie was sure Auntie knew she had come to a decision but Auntie was a great respecter of persons, even small persons, and she asked no questions. Instead she had lit the fire and there was roast chicken for supper as if it were Christmas but Lottie could not eat it. Afterwards they sat by the fire sewing on the last of the name tapes that had been rushed through, on Lottie's – to them – large number of clothes.

'A gross of nametapes! A gross is a dozen dozen!' said Auntie. 'And we've used most of them. Thank God we got a grant.'

To most girls school uniforms are something to be endured but Lottie had never had clothes as good as these: a well-cut grey skirt, white blouses, two scarlet cardigans and the cloak Auntie had thought extravagant, green lined with scarlet. She had two suitcases with more of the unimaginable riches Auntie had studied on the list: under-clothes, pyjamas, a dressing gown – Lottie had always managed with her raincoat – as well as things that belonged only to this particular school: leotards, white cotton socks, white knitted crossovers to keep shoulders and chests warm, a dirndl skirt for character dancing – Auntie had made Lottie's and sewn it with bright rick-rack braid – and a scarlet track suit. 'How we're going to get you there, I don't know,' said Auntie, but that had been solved: Lion had offered to drive them to Queen's Chase.

'I'd quite like to look at this dump of yours,' he told Lottie. 'I might have gone there myself.'

When the sewing was finished they sat looking at the fire. Prince had eaten most of Lottie's chicken and now was comfortably asleep with his head on Auntie's shoe. Lottie watched him for a moment and one last rebel thought flared up in her. Suddenly, 'I don't have to go,' she said.

'You do.' Auntie looked squarely at Lottie. 'Did you know, Lottie, that before she died, Madame told me you were a better dancer than Henrietta?'

'Than *Henrietta*! Me?' Lottie's control broke; she flung herself into Auntie's arms crying hysterically.

Auntie held her close, patting her as if she were baby Lottie again not this nightmare Charlotte. Then when the crying had stopped and Lottie lay back exhausted against her shoulder Auntie said what she had never said before: 'I'm sure it will all turn out for the best. For the best,' said Auntie firmly.

Next morning Auntie left for work as usual. 'I'll be back at twelve.'

Mr Soper had asked them to a 'send off' lunch party. 'In a restaurant!' Auntie had exclaimed.

'Only that little run-down Italian place in the High Street,' said Mrs Cuthbert who had not been invited.

Mr Soper had asked Miss Dorcas and Miss Dora, and, from Holbein's, Zanny and Emil – Hilda and Lion were to come in for coffee. Lottie was to wear her uniform to show them, 'And the cloak,' Auntie stroked its folds.

It had all become immediate and real. It should have been exciting but as Auntie left for Holbein's she put her hand on Lottie's shoulder. 'Dearie, I'll try and manage for Prince – somehow.'

'You needn't,' Lottie should have said but could not. 'I'll tell Auntie when it's done.'

Resolutely she washed the breakfast things, stripped

her bed, tidied her room. Then she put on her old rain-coat – it looked unbelievably shabby beside the new clothes. 'Come,' she said sternly to Prince.

The evening before, waiting for Auntie to come in, Lottie had sat down at her desk – Henrietta's old desk – and written out 'Prince's Programm' – she was not sure how to spell it:

Breakfast . . . . . . . . . . . . . . . . . . . . . milk and biscuits
Midle day . . . . . . . . . . . . . . . . . . . . meat, brown bread
Supper . . . . . . . . . . . . . . . . . . . . . meat, brown bread
Out every two hours – newspapers.
Please buy him a bed – his box is too smale

Then she wrote a note:

Dear Violetta,
Please will you have Prince as your very own. I have to go to bording school and can't keep him. I know you love him, he'll be happy with you and you *must* take him for a walk every day.
Love Lottie.

She put it in an envelope, threaded a ribbon through it to hang round Prince's neck; then she packed his ball, a slipper Auntie had sacrificed for him, his towel and the brush she had bought, his bowl marked DOG and put them all into a plastic bag. She fetched his collar and lead – he was bouncing so much with glee at going out she could hardly put them on. 'Come,' she said to him sternly.

Taking the door key and the bag, she peeped into the hall to make sure no one would see her, went out of the front door and along the road, the opposite way from the one that led past Mrs Cuthbert's window.

Auntie had given her pocket money. 'Five pounds,' Lottie had said in wonder.

'It's to last you till half-term,' but Lottie was going to spend some of it now and, once again, take a taxi – Prince seemed to lead to extravagance. Taxis often passed at the end of Verbena Road; she flagged one down. 'Webster Street, Soho,' she told the driver – as part of her plan she had written that down – 'but please stop at the corner.'

At the corner of Webster Street she paid off the taxi and, carrying Prince and the bag, walked to the shop – a wonderful smell came out through its doors. In the jostle of people hardly anyone noticed her though a Chinese man said, 'Pletty little dog,' and a Frenchwoman, '*Comme il est beau!*' Lottie came to the side door which was set a little back from the street. As quickly as she could – it was better to be quick – she put Prince down on the doorstep, tying him close to the foot scraper, put the bag beside him and hung the note on its ribbon round his neck.

For one moment she held his face between his soft ears, and looked into his eyes. 'Stay,' was all she could manage to say. She rang the bell and fled into the shop entrance where, among all the people, she could see and not be seen.

The door was opened by Serafina. For a moment she stood amazed, then bent and saw the note round Prince's neck. 'Vivi. Vivi,' she called up the stairs. '*Viene qui.* Come quick. Quick.' It seemed a while till Violetta came, she had to get downstairs, then, '*Guarda!* Look! Look!' cried Serafina.

Lottie did not wait to see any more. She was numbed as if all of her had gone cold; dazed, as in a bad dream, she walked to catch the familiar bus she always took back and forth to the bead shop.

Auntie came back at twelve and almost at once, 'Prince?' she asked. 'Where's Prince?'

'He's gone. He won't be here any more.' Lottie made her voice gruff. 'I've given him to Violetta.'

'Given him ... to ... Violetta.' Auntie stood stock still. Then, 'Oh, you poor lamb!'

'Auntie, don't. Don't talk about it at all.'

It should have been marvellous – and it was marvellous. 'The little restaurant wasn't run down,' Auntie told Mrs

Cuthbert. 'We had delicious spaghetti and pink wine. I didn't know wine could be pink.'

'Rosé d'Anjou,' Mr Soper said airily. This was a new kind of Mr Soper.

Lottie wore her uniform. 'My, you look smart,' Mr Soper said.

'So pretty and so useful,' said Miss Dorcas.

'*Most* useful,' said Miss Dora.

They had brought presents: Miss Dorcas and Miss Dora a red leather shoulder bag. 'Oh, Lottie! Just the thing!' cried Auntie. Hilda and Lion came in for coffee and Hilda gave Lottie a good-luck mascot, a little downy owl with yellow eyes and a loop to hang him up – all the dancers at Holbein's had mascots hung on their mirrors for good luck and Lottie felt grown up. Lion gave her a five-pound note. 'No, Lion,' Auntie protested.

'Ssh! She'll need it,' said Lion.

Best of all, Zanny and Emil brought her a small gold chain bracelet. Lottie had no jewellery of any kind and was overcome. 'It belonged to Madame, long long ago,' Zanny told her.

'To Madame!' Auntie said reverently.

'Perhaps when she was Niura,' and Lottie felt the first prickle of excitement.

Then Lion looked at his watch and said, 'Time to go.'

*

Queen's Chase was seething with boys and girls. Lottie was used to a mob of children – her Hampstead school had more than four hundred – but she had never been part of the mob, always one apart, trying to keep away from the playground, never walking with anyone on her way to and from school. Now, willy-nilly, she would have to mix, be one with the others, and it was with something like pride that she showed Lion over Queen's Chase. She had only seen it once and it was surprising how much she remembered. Auntie was with the parents having tea in the Yellow Drawing Room but Lottie showed Lion the Salon, the portrait of Karsavina in the hall, the studios, her gallery dormitory, the classrooms for lessons, the yews and the lily pond – she kept away from the pets corner. 'Well, I must say,' said Lion, 'you are in luck, Lottie. No, you've earned it and you're a pedigree dancer. Do you know what a pedigree is?'

'Yes,' said Lottie, wincing as she thought of Prince.

'One of a great tradition,' said Lion with unwonted seriousness, and kissed her.

'Children,' a voice was calling, 'will you say goodbye to your parents now. New girls report to me, Mrs Gillespie your housemistress. New boys go to your wing with Mr Ormond, your housemaster.'

Lottie went with Auntie to the portico. The pink wine had made Auntie a little weepish. 'Lottie, I don't know what I'll do without you,' but on the front steps they stopped.

A car had drawn up under the portico, to Lottie, an unmistakable dark green car – and surely that was Sam who came round to open the door?

A gentleman got out, a plump gentleman in an elegant grey suit – Lottie saw the gleam of his cuff-links and the little finger ring and, yes, she had seen him before – in the hall at the senior ballet school on the day of the auditions. But how? Lottie was mystified. Why had he come with Sam? Then a boy jumped out, and, 'Oh no!' breathed Lottie. It was *the* boy.

She shrank behind Auntie, but he had seen her.

'You! The girl in the hall!' His eyes lit up with pleasure.

'You!' said Lottie in dark displeasure.

'Sir.' Sam had seen her and Auntie too. 'Sir ... Mr Ruffino, sir! This girl is Lottie. It was Lottie who gave Prince, the puppy, to Violetta.'

'Violetta is this boy's little sister,' he explained to Auntie and Lottie but, 'Puppy? Violetta?' It was obvious they were far from Mr Ruffino's thoughts.

'Prince, the puppy,' prompted Sam.

'Ah! Our Cavalier spaniel!' cried Mr Ruffino. 'So this is Lottie, our little benefactress ... Lottie! I have long waited to meet you. Violetta is so happy.' His eyes seemed to fill with tears as he turned to Auntie. 'Violetta walks.

For years she has refused to try. Now she walks every day for Prince. I can never thank you. Oh, madam . . . '

'Miss,' said Auntie. 'Miss Tew.'

'Miss Tew, you are Lottie's aunt. Sam has told me. May I come to call on you? Indeed, I have to call regarding this so engaging little dog. To thank you and to speak with you.'

'Well, this beats all,' said Sam. Lottie thought so too.

Mr Ruffino took out his wallet and, bowing, gave Auntie a card. 'Domenico Ruffino – who is so grateful. May I present my son, Salvatore.'

Salvatore! What a name! thought Lottie as Salvatore bowed over Auntie's hand with charm.

'Auntie, it's the spider boy,' Lottie wanted to shout but Auntie was bewitched as she held the card in her hand – no one had given her a private printed card before – she was sure Mr Ruffino was a private gentleman. 'Such a handsome boy,' she crooned, 'and such good manners! But where is Violetta?'

'We had to leave her with our housekeeper. She made such a scene at her brother's going.'

'Broke her little heart,' said Sam.

'Yes, she is a tempest, that one.' Mr Ruffino was sad and took a second beautifully clean white handkerchief from his pocket to dab at his eyes. 'She so loves her brother but what can I do? Such tempest!'

'She was perfectly good with us,' Auntie defended her. 'No child could have been sweeter.'

'Ah! I think you have the touch,' said Mr Ruffino and Lottie remembered how Auntie could always manage to soothe the most recalcitrant and nervous dancer.

'Perhaps Vivi could come sometimes and visit you. You will be lonely without Miss Lottie.' Mr Ruffino had seen Auntie's red eyes and spoke gently. 'I too without Salvatore but I am much pleased with this coincidence.'

'Yes,' said Auntie, cheered. 'How lovely, Lottie, to know you have a friend here on your very first day.'

'I only know,' Lottie wanted to cry, 'I have given Prince to the sister of the spider boy.'

# CHAPTER VIII

When Lottie went with the other new girls to Mrs Gillespie she forgot about Salvatore because Irene was there.

'I've been waiting for you.' Irene was surrounded by a phalanx of girls. 'Girls, this is Charlotte my best friend. Charlotte, this is Priscilla, my best friend.' Sybil, Anne-Marie, Abigail, best friends. Though Irene had only been at Queen's Chase for half an hour it seemed she had many best friends but Lottie simply thought Irene was the leader – naturally.

Mrs Gillespie called Lottie and introduced her to a fourth-year girl, immensely tall and beautiful in Lottie's eyes. 'This is Charlotte Tew, Angela. Charlotte, Angela's going to be your guide.'

Every new boy or girl had a guide for their first term, not always a willing one, but now, 'Wasn't that Lionel Ray who brought you?' Angela was agog.

'Lion? Yes.'

'You call him Lion! Then you know him well.'

'Of course, he was at Holbein's too.' Angela was immediately and specially kind to Lottie: she showed her where her bed was in that strange gallery dormitory.

'Such a narrow little bed!' Irene's mother, Mrs St Charles, said in dismay – she had managed to stay when the other parents left – and, 'Where do they keep their things?'

'They have a share in a cupboard, and two drawers,' said Mrs Gillespie, 'and this locker beside their beds.'

'Such a small locker!' and, seeing Mrs St Charles's – and Irene's – dismayed faces, 'The children are here to learn to be dancers,' Mrs Gillespie said it seriously. 'When dancers go on tour they have to get used to sleeping in all kinds of narrow beds, bunks in ships, berths in trains, uncomfortable lodgings. Again, in the theatre when they come to dress and make up with perhaps forty other girls, they can use only the smallest space and must hang up their costumes carefully or they'll be in trouble with the wardrobe mistress' – 'Indeed yes,' Auntie would have said – and, 'Bring as little as you can,' Mrs Gillespie said as she had so often said before when she cautioned the new girls. That was easy for Lottie: the only things she had beside her clothes were a stage photograph of Henrietta as the Carnation Fairy in *The Sleeping Beauty* ballet and Hilda's good-luck owl, which she hung over her bed.

Angela helped her unpack, showed her where to find schoolrooms and ballet studios. 'It's confusing, so at first I'll come and take and fetch you.' Then, 'Mrs Challoner wants to see you,' said Angela. 'I'll take you to her study.'

Mrs Challoner asked at once. 'Prince? What did you do?'

'What you said, asked Zanny.' Lottie swallowed. 'Madame gave Glinka away.'

'Because?'

'She had to go away too.'

'Like you.' Mrs Challoner did not ask any more; she put her hand on Lottie's shoulder and said, 'Brave girl.' Lottie almost said, 'But I've given him to ...' when Mrs Challoner went on. 'The only thing for you to do now, Charlotte,' said Mrs Challoner, 'is to be extremely busy. In fact you'll have to work hard in lessons to keep up. You've made Prince safe, that's the important thing. Now let him be and get on with everything.'

'And one – and two, and three and four ... down – and up – down ...'

'Right! Count four. Prepare. Good. Don't pull on the *barre*, Sybil. Use your muscles to hold you up. Bend, two, three, stretch five … six … *Pull up*, stomach in, tail in, ribs down, head up. *Up!* Use your eyes.'

There were eleven small girls in pale blue leotards, pale pink belts to show they were first years, pale pink soft dancing shoes. 'Not *pointe*,' said Irene. 'But I've been on *pointe*.'

'Then you shouldn't have been. You're not ready.' Miss McKenzie said it sharply. 'An over-ambitious teacher,' she said, discussing Irene with Miss Hurley.

All of them, except Priscilla who had short hair, had a knot on the top of their heads, or in a coronal of plaits. 'I need to see your necks,' said Miss McKenzie. Irene's curls kept escaping. 'Well, you keep shaking your head.'

'Round your arms. Listen to the music. No! No! *No!* Why do you think we have a pianist? *Use* the music, fill it out. Let it help you. Don't just count it, *feel* it.'

'Prepare. One, and a two, and a three, and a four …'

Music seemed to ring in Lottie's ears, from slow waltzes to quick double four–four time; it beat in her head, day and night, except that at night she was too tired for it to last long. When she woke, in her white bed among eleven other white beds, she wondered at first where she was and then lay marvelling that she should be there at all. Almost at once, though, as she thought over yesterday's work, it began again.

'And one and two and three – turn – four.' Music. Music. Voices ...

'Does *every* class have to start with *pliés*?' Irene complained. Irene, it seemed, had been allowed to dance as she chose. '*Pliés! Pliés!*'

'It has to. They stretch us and make us turn out,' and, as if to confirm what Lottie said, 'Knees over toes, please, girls, in a *beautiful* turn out.' That was the young French ballet teacher, Mamzelly, coaxing, 'Down, then up and stretch, *chérie*. Str-etch. Good! Good girl.'

The first-year girls had three ballet teachers – although they were married they were all called 'Miss': Miss McKenzie, the senior, charming French Mademoiselle Giroux whom everyone called Mamzelly, and old Miss Hurley – 'She's the worst,' the second years warned the firsts.

They were not the only dance teachers. The small boys started with Miss McKenzie but there were two masters for the older ones.

Another master came for folk dancing on Saturday mornings – something new to Lottie who loved it, particularly when, at its end, came the *grande promenade*, each boy taking two girls and circling the room, the girls showing off their brightly coloured skirts.

What impressed Lottie most at Queen's Chase was the seriousness of the teachers: they made Hilda seem almost light-hearted. 'Like this, girls,' Miss McKenzie would say. 'Think that you're drawing a line with your toe on the floor. *Tendu*, now the half circle, *en dehors*. What does that mean, Sybil?' Sybil looked blank. 'Charlotte?'

'Circle outwards.' This was where Lottie scored; she had grown up with the language of ballet, French.

'I always forget what hard work it is with the new children,' Miss McKenzie said. 'From remembering their names! You not only have to show them everything but *tell* them everything, except Charlotte Tew.'

'Clever clogs,' said Irene, and Lottie quickly learned not to put herself forward.

Miss Hurley was perhaps the most particular. 'Anne-Marie, your big toe isn't pointing.'

How did Miss Hurley know? wondered Lottie. Anne-Marie's big toe was hidden inside her shoe but Miss Hurley was stretching and arching Anne-Marie's foot until, 'Ouch!' cried Anne-Marie.

'Watch that hand, Sybil. Joanna, don't wriggle your shoulders. We don't want to look like this, do we?' Miss Hurley could give a wonderful imitation of St Vitus' dance which set the whole class laughing, 'And taught you something,' said Miss Hurley, laughing too.

Miss Hurley's stampings were not, as Madame Holbein's had been, from temper but to get attention and Lottie, used to Madame's and Hilda's exasperations, asked herself, 'How does she find the patience when she must have taught hundreds of girls?'

'Simply because I have taught hundreds of little girls,' Miss Hurley would have said if Lottie had had the courage to ask her. 'The wonder is – and I never cease to wonder at it – that each one is different. Take you, Charlotte, Irene and Priscilla.'

'It's all so easy,' Irene complained.

'It's all so difficult,' said Priscilla.

'You'd think we'd never learned dancing before,' moaned Irene.

'We haven't. Not like this,' Priscilla, contented, said. Some of them – including Irene – had to unlearn, which was even harder and, 'I ache,' said Priscilla. 'My back and feet!'

'I ache all over.'

'I never ached like this in *my* dancing classes,' said Irene.

In a strange way Lottie welcomed the aching. 'I think it shows our bodies are learning too,' she told Irene.

'My body doesn't want to.' Irene was emphatic.

'Nor mine,' Lottie often wanted to say. 'And when you have to think of what every inch of you is doing, as well as remembering the steps, *and* listen to the music, it's impossible.'

'It isn't,' said Miss McKenzie. 'It will come, not in five

minutes, not in a year, or three or four years, but it will come,' and Lottie believed her. She could not see how any child at Queen's Chase could fail to be a dancer.

For one thing, she, who had looked after not only herself but Auntie, had never dreamed that so many grown-up people could spend their whole day, sometimes half their night, caring for children. And they really do care, thought Lottie.

Some of these grown-ups had little to do with dancing, yet were tightly bound up with it: people like Mrs Gillespie and Sister, and the boys had Mr Ormond, and a matron, Polly Walsh, who seemed too young to be called Matron. There was the housekeeper, Mrs Meredith – Mrs Merry to the children – who was so careful over their meals. 'Did you like the apple tart, Charlotte?' 'Was the fish nice?' For very pride Lottie had to hide how glorious she thought they were.

Mrs Merry worked with Chef, 'a real chef in a chef's hat,' Lottie told Auntie. Helped by two 'counter ladies', he served from a big counter just outside the dining hall and kept a watch on what each girl or boy took on their trays.

'Not just chips,' Chef would say sternly, 'a green vegetable as well, or you can have a salad.'

There were other ladies who cleaned the house – beyond making her bed Lottie did not do any housework.

Clean clothes appeared twice a week, neatly folded on her locker, 'For me, Lottie!' She remembered how her back and wrist used to ache from ironing. Every Friday she and Irene shampooed each other's hair, giving it a thorough brushing afterwards so that Lottie's dark straight locks began to have a new sheen.

Quite apart from the hairwashing, just to be in the same place as Irene was, for Lottie, heaven; to be admitted more and more so that she really did appear to be her best friend. 'You must come and spend the weekend with us,' Irene told her. 'My ma wants to talk to you about Holbein's. Would you like to?'

'Would I like!'

It seemed everyone was smiling on Lottie.

Above everyone, of course, was Mrs Challoner – some of the smaller boys and girls thought Queen's Chase belonged to Mrs Challoner. She was the bridge for girls and boys alike between the closed world of ballet and the world outside and was so concerned with the least of them that they felt they could go to her at any time. Not that she was easy-going: she was strict but even when she was dealing out judgement, she had a twinkle in her eye. Lottie had never met a grown-up who had the least vestige of a twinkle; she began to love Mrs Challoner. Under Mrs Challoner was an array of school teachers – Lottie thought she could have done without them.

'Don't you know *anything?*' asked outspoken Irene and, 'At this school you went to,' Mrs Challoner had to say, 'I don't think you paid enough attention.'

'I didn't pay any attention,' would have been the truthful answer. How could she, Lottie, have paid attention? Not only looking after the flat and shopping, doing Auntie's errands and three times a week dancing classes, but, 'You don't spell cloud like that,' said Priscilla who helped her – Lottie had written 'clowd' – and, 'Look, that's a map you have to trace.'

Angela, too, still watched over her, though more severely. 'Don't you know even the auxiliary French verbs, Charlotte? Come along now. I'll hear you.'

'*Je suis* ...'

'Not swee. *Je suis, tu es, il est* ...' and, 'Good girl,' said Angela at the end, just as Miss McKenzie or Miss Hurley said when Lottie had sweated to hold her leg higher without a wobble in an *arabesque.*

Mamzelly said, '*Très bien.* Bravo!' and Lottie glowed.

'You know,' Miss McKenzie said to Miss Hurley, 'that little girl is getting to be positively pretty.'

'Perhaps now she's settling down to being a child,' said Mrs Challoner, 'not an anxious little hen.'

As he had said he would, Mr Ruffino came to call on Auntie.

She had come home early for once and was missing Lottie: the flat seemed so empty. She put on the television but, as it was part of a serial, she could not make any sense of it. She tried another channel which yielded a chat show that jarred, another showed African children in famine. 'Oh dear,' said Auntie, 'I suppose I ought to watch that,' but she switched off. She decided to give herself a treat and light the fire; then she sat beside it, wondering what Lottie was doing at that moment. Having a good supper, she thought with gratitude. She did not hear the car draw up and the bell startled her. Who at this hour? Then, peeping through the curtains, she saw, above the basement railings, the shape of the big green car. Sam, she thought, with a message, but no, it was Mr Ruffino. Mr Ruffino!

'May I come in?'

'Please. Please.' Auntie was flustered. He came in, taking off his hat. Once again he was all in grey. He took in the firelight, the empty room, Auntie's forlorn chair. 'You are missing your little niece, I think.'

The sympathy in his voice, he had a deep rich voice, made tears start in Auntie's eyes. 'Yes,' she said. 'Oh, forgive me. It's just that Lottie ... but please, please sit down.'

'I, too, miss Salvatore, bad boy as he is. Violetta is inconsolable, or she would be had she not this wonderful gift of Prince. He is why I want to talk to you, Miss Tew.'

'First, may I make you some tea?' But do Italians drink tea? Probably they like coffee but, 'I'm afraid I have nothing else to offer you,' she said.

'Tea would be excellent.' Making it for someone else is quite different from making it for oneself and Auntie was quite cheered by the time she set the tray on a small table by the fire. She had the rest of a chocolate cake she had bought for Lottie's farewell. Mr Ruffino drew up his chair and took a large slice. 'This is good, very good at the end of a day's work.'

'That's what I think.' Auntie smiled and nodded.

After a second cup and another slice of cake, he wiped his hands on a fine white handkerchief and said, 'Now to business.'

'Business? What business?'

'This business of the little dog.'

'There isn't any business about Prince. We are just glad for your little daughter to have him.'

'So am I but, Miss Tew, did you know Charlotte put him on our doorstep, rang the bell and ran away?'

'Poor lamb! She couldn't face it. *Poor* lamb!'

'Yes, but we could not even say thank you.'

'If you'll have him and love him and look after him, that is all the thanks we need. Lottie told me, too, that Violetta refused to try and walk but she walks willingly with Prince.'

'Yes, that makes it a double gift but—'

'No "buts", Mr Ruffino, please. What is done is done. It will be best for Lottie, Violetta too – all of us. Please don't upset it.'

'Indeed I won't but, Miss Tew, that is a pedigree well-bred little dog. I can't let Violetta accept such a valuable present. You must let me purchase him.'

'Purchase? You mean buy him? Oh, no, Mr Ruffino, we couldn't do that. I promised Lottie.'

'Then at least let me reimburse what you paid for him.'

'Paid? We didn't pay anything. You see Lottie found him.'

'*Found* him?'

'Yes, in the street. No one was with him and he was hurt, bruised, his little back paw. Lottie took him to the People's Dispensary for Sick Animals. A kind lady helped her. The vet told her to take him home and keep him warm and quiet, so she did.'

'But . . . a dog like that! This is most peculiar.'

'I suppose it is. I suppose we ought to have taken him to the police. I just didn't think. Oh, is it stealing, Mr Ruffino?' She raised anguished eyes to his face.

'Usually to steal one must have intent.' Mr Ruffino was smiling. 'I don't think you – or Lottie – had any such intent.'

'Then you don't think . . . I ought to tell the police?'

'No,' Mr Ruffino said firmly. 'In any case they would say it is too late. Let it be a secret between you and me and Lottie. And yes, I accept for Violetta. I think, Miss Tew, we haven't yet begun to know what that little dog will do.'

'I walked past three times,' said Mrs Cuthbert. 'Of course, I've seen the car before.'

'I'm sure you have.'

'It's that little Italian girl and the dog.' Mrs Cuthbert was not to be put off. Auntie had told Mrs Cuthbert how Lottie had given Prince to Violetta.

'*Lottie* gave him, not I,' said Auntie.

'Sensible for once.'

'Yes, and, Edna, you will please not talk about it to her.'

Now, 'The lame little girl wasn't there,' Mrs Cuthbert was saying, 'only the gentleman.'

'He came to see me about Prince.'

'And stayed two hours?'

'I know.' Auntie was quite serene.

# CHAPTER IX

'Salvatore Ruffino', said Mrs Challoner, 'is a most dis-ruptive boy.'

'He seems to want to be diabolical,' said Polly Walsh.

Nothing seemed to delight Salvatore more than spoil-ing any kind of peace: if two boys were playing chess he would come quietly and upset the board; if anyone were painting, he would knock the water over the picture. He put salt in the sugar bowls on the dining tables and, knowing Mrs Merry's dread of mice, he brought three dead ones back from home at the weekend – there were plenty of mice in Soho – and put them on a plate in the refrigerator for her to find.

'Another of Salvatore's stupid jokes,' said Lottie loftily.

'But why?' asked Mrs Challoner. 'They all love Mrs Merry.'

'I think he has some grudge against the world,' said

Polly Walsh. 'Also he wants to make his mark with the other boys.'

'He goes the worst way about it.'

The boys had disliked him from the first: it was his luscious good looks, his boasting, especially about his papa.

'Who's your papa?' he asked Desmond.

'Lord Cherston,' said Desmond whose father happened to be an earl. Salvatore was unabashed.

'Bet he hasn't a car-hire business with a hundred cars and a restaurant *and* a delicatessen.'

'You were a silly to tell them that,' Polly told him, and sure enough the children were soon calling him Macaroni and Pasta Pest. Pest was right, yet he intrigued them.

To begin with, the way he had got himself to Queen's Chase was as unbelievable to the other children as it had been to Lottie. 'You mean you never had a dancing lesson until now?' said Desmond.

'Never,' said Salvatore. 'I used to go to a day school near the Theatre Royal and often some of our boys took part in an opera or ballet when children were needed who didn't have to dance or sing, just act a little. Then *The Dream* was put on' – *The Dream* was a ballet taken from *A Midsummer Night's Dream* – and as always a boy was needed for the Indian changeling. 'I'm so dark I could be an Indian and so small and light I could be a fairy changeling – see how light I am,' and Salvatore did a leap, inordinately high and landed without a sound, 'so they chose me. Ennis Glyn was dancing Titania, Yuri Koszorz Oberon. Oberon had to throw me across the stage.' As he told this Salvatore changed before their eyes into an intensely earnest boy who said, 'It was then that I knew I would be a dancer.'

'And they took you! Why?'

'Because I have such talent.'

'Oh dear! Saying that's not going to do him any good,' said Polly.

The second-year boys had already noted that Mr Max, who did not usually teach the smallest boys – he was the senior ballet master – now visited the first-year boys' class far more often than he had done in their time and, 'It's aeons since I had a boy like this,' Desmond heard Miss McKenzie say.

What the children found strangest of all was that Salvatore did not seem to care in the least that he was unpopular. 'Nobody likes you,' Priscilla told him. Salvatore shrugged and whistled as if to say, 'I like myself.' He led a blithe life of his own on which it seemed no one made any impression. When Mr Ormond lost patience with him, which he seldom did with any of the boys, on the evening of the day he gave Salvatore his worst scolding and punishment – 'No sweets or comics for two weeks' – Polly caught him making Mr Ormond an apple-pie bed.

'I could hardly keep a straight face,' Polly told Mrs Challoner, 'I must say I've longed sometimes to make Mr Ormond an apple-pie bed. And it *is* hard for him.' Polly meant Salvatore not Mr Ormond. 'If you've been spoiled it isn't easy to get unspoiled.'

'Yes, look at Irene St Charles,' said Mrs Challoner.

Discipline at Queen's Chase was strict. 'It has to be or the children could never get through what they have to do,' said Mrs Challoner, 'which is to work twice as hard as children in ordinary schools.'

Salvatore, it seemed, had never had any discipline and, 'I don't like the hours,' he explained to Mrs Challoner.

He hated being woken by the bell and having to get up at once, otherwise Desmond who was monitor in the dormitory pulled the bedclothes off him.

'Make my own bed?' Salvatore had asked in astonishment.

'Well, who do you think will do it for you?' asked Polly. 'If you're going to be a dancer you'll have to do everything for yourself.' That aspect of dancing had not occurred to Salvatore.

'Time-tables mean you have to be on time,' Mr Ormond told him. Salvatore could not get used to that.

'Late again!' said one school teacher after another – he was never late for dancing, Mrs Challoner noted.

'Go back to the end of the queue, you little twerp,' a big boy would order as Salvatore tried to edge in front of the long line of boys and girls waiting with their trays for lunch; it had not occurred to the big boy that Salvatore had never stood in a queue before.

Worst of all was night time. 'Bed at *half past eight! Lights out at nine!* But ... that's just the time when I used to go out,' he cried in dismay.

'Out!' The others stared.

It was Polly who discovered that, at home, when Mr Ruffino and Serafina thought Salvatore was in bed, he used to creep out leaving a dummy pillow figure, escape through a bathroom window and down the fire-escape to wander in the streets. 'Those streets!' said Polly with a shudder. 'God knows what he saw and learned.'

Jake and some of the big boys encouraged Salvatore to tell. Salvatore was flattered and, 'I expect he makes it highly lurid,' said Mr Ormond wearily. He could tell ghost stories too, terrifying the younger boys, especially the youngest, Thomas.

'You know that dark place in the hall just outside the Salon,' Salvatore would begin, 'and the big mirror that hangs there? If you went at midnight and looked into it, the mirror would crack from side to side and blood would come out.' Salvatore's eyes glistened. The term was getting on for winter and by half past four, one of the times of Thomas's dancing class, the hall was dark. Thomas had to pass the mirror and shook with fear.

'Don't be thick,' Desmond said. 'Ask Mr Salvatore why the mirror isn't cracked in the morning and who mopped up the blood?'

'It's *supernatural*,' said Salvatore, making that a fearsome word.

Polly could have told that Salvatore could be frightened too. He did not like the wide spaces of the Park, especially after dark and at night lay awake, 'Listening to the dark,' she said. The first time he heard an owl hoot he was out of bed and into Polly's room trembling.

'It's a ghost. It says "Who? Who? Who did that? Who did this?" That's always me. Oh, Polly' – he always called her Polly – 'oh, Polly, does it mean I'm going to die? *Die!*' No one would have recognised the hard little braggart of the day.

'He's impervious,' Mr Ormond said in despair.

'The imp part is right,' Polly agreed. 'I think it will always be there but you mean he doesn't feel. It may astonish you, but I think Salvatore feels more deeply than almost any of the boys. That's why he behaves as he does. He knows he's a misfit.'

'Except for dancing.' Mrs Challoner said it thought-fully.

Irene asked Lottie for the weekend. 'Well, I don't know,' said Auntie, who had to give her permission. 'You ought not to go because I don't see how we can ask Irene back.' But Lottie had set her heart on going and it really did seem she was Irene's best friend when she found herself in Lowndes Square.

The grandeur of the spacious flat was quite different from Violetta's. 'Far more beautiful,' said Lottie.

'It's only a flat.' Irene dismissed it. 'We really live in Australia.' But there were polished parquet floors, rugs that Irene said were Persian; the drawing room had small gilded chairs, cabinets like Auntie's but filled with fine porcelain, a shining grand piano and a harp – Mrs St Charles played both.

There was a cook, Mrs Wilson, and a maid who seemed to be called by her surname, Bentley. They did not appear to be Irene's friends but were nice to Lottie. 'Mrs Wilson's so kind.'

'Funny old thing,' said Irene. 'I 'spect she's sorry for you.'

'Why should she be sorry?' flared Lottie. Indeed Mrs St Charles, like Madame, seemed to think she was lucky and asked her endlessly about Holbein's, particularly about Madame.

'And to think she taught you herself! You were there from a baby. Oh, Irene! How I wish I could have given you that.'

'I wouldn't have said "thank you",' said Irene's look.

They went to the Park, to the shops, to the cinema – Lottie's first visit to one – and to a play at the theatre, that was new too.

'Ma wanted us to go to the ballet,' said Irene, 'but I told her we had enough of that already.'

Three or four times a term Queen's Chase boys and girls, even the first years, were taken to the ballet. Seats were reserved for them in the gallery. So, 'I'm glad you chose a play,' said Lottie.

There was, however, one difficulty about the play.

'We're going to have dinner out so wear dresses,' Mrs St Charles had said.

Lottie had only her one good dress, which she was growing out of; in any case it was very different from Irene's black velvet skirt and bolero worn over a Chinese silk blouse. She saw Irene looking at her dress. 'You can wear one of mine if you like.'

Lottie did not know what made her suddenly still nor what made her say, 'Thank you but I'd rather wear mine.'

'You will remember to write a thank-you letter,' Auntie said when Lottie told her all about it on the telephone. Lottie felt she could never say thank you enough.

'Auntie,' Lottie said on the telephone – she tried to ring Auntie up every week. 'This afternoon we were put on *pointe* though we only stood on them for a moment at a time. We had to exercise in them, first on the floor, then walking and running on them flat – they did feel funny. Then at the *barre*, we went up on them, for a few seconds, then up and down, up, down.'

'Pooh! I was on *pointe* long ago without all this fuss,' said Irene.

'Fuss!' said Miss Hurley. 'A child's foot could be injured for life. Do you want to have a deformed foot – all distorted? Don't let me catch you doing silly things on your own.'

Lottie often trembled for her adored Irene.

'Where is Irene?' Miss Hurley asked one afternoon as she surveyed the class of little girls. 'She can't be ill or Sister would have told me. Where is she? Yes, Sybil?'

'I think she said she doesn't feel like dancing today, Miss Hurley.'

'*Doesn't feel like dancing?*' Miss Hurley's breath seemed almost taken away. 'Go and fetch her *at once*.' When Irene came, 'As you don't feel like dancing you had better not dance at all. You will attend classes and sit on the side for a week.'

'Pooh!' Irene told the others. 'It will be a nice rest.'

'Oh, Irene!' Lottie expostulated. 'If you told Miss Hurley you were sorry—' but Irene rounded on Lottie.

'You're such a good little donkey! You only do what you're told. You never do anything on your own.'

That stung Lottie. Irene to speak to her like that! 'Charlotte's besotted with that girl,' Miss McKenzie told Mrs Challoner. 'I'm not a donkey,' Lottie flung at Irene. 'I do do things on my own. Look how I got Prince.'

'How did you get Prince?' Irene only knew that Charlotte adored a little dog she had had to leave. 'Well, I left my pony in Australia and – how did you get Prince?' she challenged.

A wild desire to boast filled Lottie. 'I'll never tell anyone, not even Auntie,' she had vowed yet now she did not hesitate. 'Promise you won't tell,' she said.

'Promise.'

'May I die if I lie.'

'May I die if I lie.'

'I was by this pet shop,' began Lottie. 'I often used to stop there and look at the pets, and a big boy . . . ' By the time Lottie had finished with him the boy had become a giant. 'I went after him, only me. I tripped him up. I flung my case . . . he ran away. I rescued Prince and I took him to a vet . . . ' Lottie had left out the kind lady – it was I, I, I. 'The vet told me to keep him quiet and warm so I got a taxi and I took him home,' finished Lottie. As she told it, it could not have been more dramatic and Irene was thrilled.

'I didn't know you had it in you,' she said.

Salvatore unwisely started baiting the girls: he fastened Sybil's plaits to the back of her chair with a drawing pin while she was eating. Salvatore was deft-fingered; the drawing pin came out but the jerk to her plaits hurt when Sybil got up. He put gravel in their house shoes while they were dancing, and another of his jokes, a snake this time, in Anne-Marie's locker. He offered them chocolates made of *papier-mâché* but he always excepted Lottie though he made her a special target, courting her in a stately Italian way that embarrassed her acutely. 'Pasta Pest,' she hissed. He even invaded the girls' table at meals to try to sit next to her and on Saturday morning's folk dancing – the only time boys and girls danced together – when it was time for the *grande promenade*, he would dash across the room and seize her. Usually she managed to free herself but once Mr Belton who took the class, commanded, 'Charlotte, you and Priscilla dance with Salvatore,' and they were arm in arm. Lottie had to admit that promenading with Salvatore was different from doing it with any other boy: there was a verve and dash about him which was infectious but at the end he laughed as he let her go. 'You liked that, didn't you?'

'I hated it,' said Lottie.

'I think Salvatore's keen on you,' Irene told her, not without envy.

'He isn't,' said Lottie fiercely. 'I won't have it.'

'Why won't you leave Charlotte alone?' said Irene.

The first-year girls were waiting for their weekly class with Miss McKenzie when Salvatore, who should not have been anywhere near, came butting in. 'Leave her alone,' said Irene.

He surveyed them. 'You're all jealous.'

'Jealous?'

'Yes, because she's the best dancer among you lot. That's why I chose her.'

'*Chose me!*' Lottie nearly choked. But Irene was crimson with indignation. She gave Salvatore a slap across the face.

Salvatore leapt at her but even he, strong as he was, had no chance against ten girls. In a minute they had him on the ground, two of them knelt on him pummelling him. Anne-Marie and Sybil held his legs and pinched them; Priscilla pulled his jersey over his head. Lottie stood aghast, too horrified to join in.

It might have turned more vicious but Miss McKenzie came to take the class. '*Girls!* What *are* you doing? Get up at once. At *once*. Have you completely forgotten where you are?'

Panting but triumphant they got up leaving Salvatore on the floor.

'And you?' said Miss McKenzie to him. 'What are you doing here? No,' to the girls, 'I don't want to hear any tales,' and to Salvatore, 'Go back where you should be. I shall report this to Mr Ormond.'

Salvatore stood up, pulling his jersey down; flushed and dishevelled, he had red marks on his face and neck and legs, his hair had fallen over his eyes; he was furious. 'Just you wait,' he told the girls and, 'Just *you* wait,' he said to Miss McKenzie.

Next week the girls came to get their shoes for Miss McKenzie's class. They kept them in linen bags in pigeon holes in the changing room: their soft dancing shoes, heeled ones for character dancing and their new precious pale pink satin *pointe* shoes, which they had meticulously darned under Mamzelly's watchful eyes and sewn on ribbons.

They stopped: none of the left-foot *pointe* shoes were there – except Lottie's.

'If only he had taken mine too,' mourned Lottie. It made her feel horridly conspicuous.

'Only the *left* shoes?' asked Mrs Challoner and had to say, 'One has to admit it's a neat revenge.' All the girls' ballet teachers gathered when Mrs Challoner sent for Salvatore.

'Salvatore, where did you put them?'

'Threw them in the pond,' said Salvatore sweetly.

'*Mon Dieu!*' screamed Mamzelly.

'I don't believe that for a moment,' said Mrs Challoner and, 'Mr Ruffino,' she told Salvatore's papa who had been summoned, 'that boy held out against all of us grown-ups. It wasn't until evening that his matron, Miss Walsh, found the shoes in a pillow case under the pillow in his bed.' Mrs Challoner had to say too, 'Mr Ruffino, there has been trouble ever since Salvatore came.'

'You mean Salvatore, my Salvatore, did all these things?'

'Didn't he do them at his other school?'

'Nobody told me.' Mr Ruffino passed his hand over what was left of his hair as if he were bewildered. 'It is so difficult,' he told Mrs Challoner. 'Children without a mother and I am not a young father when it might be easier to understand. Serafina, my housekeeper, spoils them, and I so busy with the shop and restaurant, the car business. I try, but Salvatore, he does not seem to care.'

'I think there is one way of making Salvatore care,' said Mrs Challoner. 'Suspend him from dancing.'

'If I had my way he would be expelled,' said Mr Ormond. 'He's nothing but a nuisance.'

'Nothing!' For once Miss McKenzie was shrill. 'I've

told you I haven't had a boy of such promise for years.'

'Just because the brat is good at dancing.'

'May I remind you the reason he is here *is* his dancing—'

Mrs Challoner intervened. 'All the same, he must behave. I'm sure Ennis would agree?'

Ennis Glyn saw Salvatore herself.

'You mean I'm not to dance!' Salvatore could not believe his ears.

'Why should you dance?' asked Ennis Glyn. 'You show no respect for other dancers – or for their property.' She tried not to let her lips twitch when she thought of the left shoes. 'So you will be suspended from all dancing for a fortnight.'

'It should be a month,' Mrs Challoner had said.

But again Miss McKenzie had cried, 'Oh no!'

'A fortnight,' said Ennis Glyn.

'Two whole weeks!'

'As far as we are concerned it might have been for ever. I was going to ask your father to take you away.'

'For a few little mistakes?' Salvatore was shocked.

'Added up they are not little. You have shown yourself to be disruptive, without respect for people and property. If it happens once again, Salvatore, that will be the end of your time with us.' Miss Glyn spoke very seriously. 'As it is you are lucky it's only two weeks.'

Salvatore was appalled. 'What shall I do?' he asked piteously.

'*Try* and behave. Also, you will apologise to each of those girls,' and the great Ennis Glyn asked, 'Why did you except Charlotte Tew?'

To her surprise Salvatore blushed.

He did not know that Lottie had gone to Mrs Challoner.

'You said if I had any worries ...'

'And you have a worry?'

'Yes. You know I gave Prince to Violetta?'

'Indeed I do,' said Mrs Challoner. 'It was kind and wise.'

'But was it?' The worry burst out. 'She's Salvatore's sister. Oh, I wouldn't have done it if I'd known. I'm beginning to be frightened of Salvatore. No one knows what he'll do next and Prince ...' Lottie could not go on.

'There is one person', said Mrs Challoner, 'whom Salvatore would never tease or torment and that's his little sister, nor anything belonging to her. I'm quite sure Prince is safe ...'

Lottie's face was mutinous and Mrs Challoner said, 'Charlotte, I wish you were not so set against Salvatore, it only provokes him. He will reform because he cares so much about his dancing. Come to think of it,' said Mrs Challoner, 'his dancing could be the saving of Salvatore.'

Lottie would far rather not have Salvatore saved.

# CHAPTER X

'Surely you want to go home for Christmas?' Mrs Challoner asked when Lottie came to her. She looked at Lottie's face and only saw wistfulness. She tried to hearten her: 'I expect your aunt has thought of some nice surprise.'

'I expect she hasn't.' Christmas was always one of Holbein's busiest times. 'You see, Madame had a Christmas Season.' That was when she tried out some of the younger dancers in the Company in Christmas things: *Les Patiseurs*; *Carnival*; Pavlova's *Christmas* – the children had even danced in some of them, but children or Company, dresses had to be made or contrived and Auntie was so deep in work she only took the afternoon and evening off on Christmas Day. Lottie did not know if Hilda was doing the same, perhaps not, but she did not think Auntie would really know what to do with Christmas and, 'I expect she hasn't,' said Lottie dismally.

'Then why don't you?'

'I? What could I do?'

'You have had a wonderful term, Charlotte.' That was true – except for Salvatore. If Lottie looked back there were riches, not only dancing and the eye-opening lessons, there was Irene, her blessed Irene, and, of course, Priscilla, Sybil, Anne-Marie, Abigail. She had not had child friends before, and there was Queen's Chase in all its interest and beauty, its peace, above all the sense of belonging. 'And what has your aunt had?' Mrs Challoner went on. 'She has managed without you and I don't think she has complained.'

No, now Lottie came to think about it, Auntie had not complained once.

'Why not take a little of all you've had back to her?'

'But how?'

'Suppose you made a small Christmas tree.'

'They're expensive.'

'Yes.' Mrs Challoner knew the difficulties. 'I expect Mr Lydd' – he was the school's handyman – 'could get you a little one from the plantation. We could find you some lights and the wardrobe has plenty of tinsel. You've been making Christmas tree decorations in art class.' They were from German patterns: stars and crescent moons, snowflakes, small red lanterns in shining paper. Lottie's eyes began to shine too. A Christmas tree would change the sitting room. 'Then those people who have been so kind to you ...'

'Mr Soper? Miss Dorcas and Miss Dora?'

'Yes, and Madame Holbein's old dresser.'

'Zanny.'

'What kind of a Christmas do they all have?' asked Mrs Challoner. 'Why not invite them all for dinner on Christmas Day and have a party?'

Such a bold thought made Lottie dizzy. 'That would be lovely but—'

'You mean, Auntie couldn't pay for it. Well, make it a dish party.'

'A dish ...?'

'Everyone brings something for the party. You could suggest what. Usually they're only too pleased. What do you and Auntie have for Christmas?'

'A chicken.'

'Make it a large one. After all Auntie hasn't had to keep you this term – a chicken – and sausages. I'm sure she'll agree. I'm sure, too, Miss Dorcas and Miss Dora would bring a Christmas pudding. Ask Zanny and her husband, what's his name?'

'Emil.'

'Well, Zanny and Emil, mince pies. Mr Soper would probably like to bring some wine. Mrs Cuthbert—'

'You mean ask *Mrs Cuthbert*!'

'It might well be that Mrs Cuthbert feels very lonely at Christmas. Ask her to bring a vegetable, like peas, and tangerines. You'll have quite a feast. Mrs Merry will teach you how to make bread sauce, and I have a jar of cranberry jelly I shan't use. I'm going to Paris for Christmas.'

'Presents?' Lottie hesitated. 'I've made a needle book for Auntie in sewing class.'

'If you worked hard you could make two more. Calendars for Mrs Cuthbert and Zanny. I'll show you how to make shaving balls for Mr Soper and Emil – they're just rounds of crinkly paper threaded on a string. You pull one off to wipe your razor – you can use one every day.'

'I don't think Mr Soper shaves very much,' but Lottie cheered up. 'He can have a calendar too.'

Lottie learned now what camaraderie was. 'I haven't heard of children getting their own Christmas trees,' lofty Pamela said. 'What are parents for?'

Nobody said, 'Charlotte hasn't any parents,' instead, 'I think it's splendid,' said Mrs Merry and everybody helped. Irene and Priscilla sewed in every odd moment and produced two beautiful pin cushions for Miss Dorcas and Miss Dora while Angela made a handkerchief sachet for Mrs Cuthbert. There was no pity in it all – Auntie and Lottie could not have accepted that – it was admiration. 'I think it's a great effort for a little girl,' said Mrs Merry.

She taught Lottie how to make bread sauce. 'All you need is some milk, a stale white loaf made into crumbs – half a small loaf will do – an onion, and some cloves.' Lottie had not heard of cloves but Mrs Merry gave her some and showed her how to press them into the onion. 'Simmer it all together gently until the milk is absorbed, pepper and salt, of course, then take the onion out and serve.' Mrs Merry also gave her a box of chocolates.

'You mustn't,' said Lottie shrinking back but, 'My staff is inundated with them,' said Mrs Merry and it was true that fathers and mothers, as well as the older boys and girls, showered the staff with chocolates and fruit at Christmas.

'How am I to get all these home,' Lottie worried, 'let alone my suitcases?'

She would not ask Salvatore or Sam and there was no Lion to drive her. She would have liked to ask him and Hilda to the party but they were to be dancing in Stuttgart for Christmas. 'No Holbein Christmas Season this year,' Auntie mourned.

'I shall be driving to the airport,' said Mrs Challoner. 'I'll bring you and your clobber and drop you on my way.' Queen's Chase really did seem a place of miracles, and Lottie had not dreamed she could be so excited by Christmas.

Of course there were barbs: Holbein's at Christmas

without any dancing seemed strange and, 'Do you think,' Lottie asked Miss McKenzie, 'it would be showing off if I danced a dance for them? They would so like to see how I've got on.'

'I think it would be lovely,' said Miss McKenzie. 'Let's make up a little variation and you could be a Christmas fairy. The wardrobe has all kinds of tutus and I'm sure they would sew on some spangles and make you a bodice. All you would need would be a wand and a crown. Music? We could use Brahms waltzes.'

'We haven't a piano or anybody who would play.'

'I have it on tape.'

'We haven't a cassette player.' Lottie hated to admit it.

'Really! Really!' said Pamela who had overheard. 'The Tews don't seem to have any of the things a normal child would have.'

'Pamela!' That was Miss Gillespie who had heard. 'There are thousands of children who don't have what lucky Charlotte has or, even more lucky, you.' But Lottie still winced.

In the end, Irene lent Lottie her radio-cassette player. 'I won't be taking it to Switzerland.'

Irene was going there for Christmas. Priscilla was flying to Nairobi, Anne-Marie to Delhi; of course, these were far out of Lottie's orbit but in any case she was too wound into her own new Christmas to take much notice.

She was in the library making out a list of party games when Salvatore approached her with a radiant smile and a large cardboard box which he dumped on the table in front of her. 'For your Christmas party,' he said.

The box was full of packets of raisins and nuts, dried figs, beautifully packed, a wooden box of crystallised fruit. There were red and gold crackers and a sprig of holly on top.

'No, thank you.'

'Go on, Charlotte. Take them.'

'No, thank you.'

'Why not?'

'I won't take anything from you.'

'They're not from me, they're from Papa. A thank you for Prince.'

'I don't believe your papa knows anything about them.'

'He does, he does,' but Lottie pushed the box off the table. Its packets spilled out over Salvatore's feet as, 'Shoes to you,' she said and walked away. Afterwards, oddly enough, she wished she had not said or done that.

Auntie did have surprises. As soon as Lottie opened the sitting-room door she stood transfixed in the doorway. 'Yes,' Auntie said in delight, 'Madame left me her white carpet and the velvet curtains, such a beautiful red. I had to take them up a little but they're as good as new.' Auntie had even gone to the expense of painting the walls – 'A friend of Mr Soper did them for me very reasonably' – and the once dismal room shone with colour and light, more light when Mrs Challoner brought in the Christmas tree. Then on Christmas morning there was a large heavy packet at Lottie's place and a little one. When she opened them she went pink with pleasure and surprise, 'Madame's icon!'

'Yes, she wanted you to have it and the little glass. I thought you could keep a light burning in it all Christmas.'

'A funny kind of party when you have to bring your own food!' Mrs Cuthbert began.

'It's all the rage, Edna,' said Auntie.

When Mrs Cuthbert saw what the others had brought she hastily put her packet of peas and her jelly out of sight in the kitchen, but, 'Peas go so well with chicken,' Lottie said with new tact, and gave the jelly pride of place on the pudding trolley.

'That school has improved your manners, I must say,' said Mrs Cuthbert.

The table looked festive. Hilda had given Auntie a pot of white chrysanthemums, and Lottie put sprigs of holly among the flowers. Auntie had brought out the silver that had belonged to her family: she and Lottie had spent the day polishing it; Mr Soper had provided glasses. Lottie had collected the red paper napkins that had not been used for the end-of-term party and ironed them carefully through a damp cloth so that they looked crisp and new. Several boys and girls as well as Irene and Priscilla had saved their crackers for Lottie. The Christmas tree was hung with presents and was glittering with tinsel and light. '*How* Christmassy!' chirped Miss Dorcas.

'Christmassy!' chirped Miss Dora.

'Cheerio,' said Mr Soper. He carried round glasses of sherry.

'Some people had two,' whispered Mrs Cuthbert as they all sat down to dinner.

They had just finished their first course and Lottie was taking the plates away when the bell rang. 'Dear me!' Auntie got up. 'Who could it be at this hour?'

'Carol singers.'

'Not on Christmas night.'

'You never know,' said Mrs Cuthbert. 'Amy, I should let them be.' But Auntie had gone up into the hall and opened the front door.

'Good evening, *buon Natale*. Merry Christmas,' said a man's voice: Mr Ruffino's – Lottie recognised the rolling r's. 'We just came by to wish you ...' We? Salvatore? Lottie recoiled. '... and leave the box. Salvatore wanted to make a gift to Charlotte but was too bashful.'

Pasta Creep! thought Lottie but Auntie was exclaiming, 'But how nice, how kind. You must all come in. Violetta darling – and Prince! Lottie will be *so* pleased,' and, as Lottie looked from the kitchen there was Auntie ushering them all in. Lottie went back into the kitchen and clenched her fists.

Mr Ruffino saw the table and people. 'But we disturb. We must go at once.'

'Not a bit of it.' Mr Soper had stood up. 'We can make room easily.' Mr Soper was a little above himself.

'Sherry *and* wine,' said Mrs Cuthbert.

'Of course,' said Auntie. 'Let me take your coats.'

She was interrupted by excited barks as Violetta let Prince off the lead – he had been whining and straining. Straight away he dashed into the kitchen and was jumping up at Lottie with flying ears and paws while Violetta was holding up her face to be kissed. '*Buon Natale*, Lottie.'

'I'll fetch some more chairs from my flat,' Mr Soper was saying.

'Sir, I'll help you.' That was Salvatore.

'We meant just to come by.'

Then why, thought Lottie, had Mr Ruffino brought two

bottles of wine as well as the box? She could see he had put them down by Auntie's chair. In the hubbub of introductions and excitement – 'Come and sit by us, love,' Miss Dorcas and Miss Dora were twittering to Violetta – Mr Ruffino was seated by Mrs Cuthbert who bridled as he bowed. 'This is too kind.'

'I'm afraid we have finished our first course,' Auntie began.

'Dear lady, we had our Christmas dinner, a big one, at midday. Just some sweets and nuts ... '

'I'm sure Salvatore ... Salvatore is right, isn't it?'

'Such an unusual name,' put in Mrs Cuthbert, positively cooing.

' ... could eat some pudding. Couldn't you, Salvatore?'

'Delish!' Salvatore rolled his dark eyes which made them laugh. 'I'll go and help Charlotte in the kitchen, shall I?' and got up, As if he knew the way, thought Lottie wrathfully.

'Why have you come?'

'To find a way to make you take my box.'

'Cheat. Take your papa and Violetta and Prince and go away.'

'That wouldn't be polite when your aunt has asked us to stay.'

'Creep!'

'Are you two having words?' Mr Soper had come into

the kitchen to flame the Christmas pudding. 'No quarrelling on Christmas Day.' Mr Soper was definitely above himself. 'Say pax – peace – both of you.'

'Pax,' said Salvatore promptly.

'Lottie . . .'

'Pax.' Lottie had to say it, though unwillingly.

It really was pax – and Lottie had to admit the Ruffinos added greatly to the party. The wine flowed and there was laughter, chiefly at Salvatore. 'He ate the whole of my jelly!' said Mrs Cuthbert, pleased.

'Yes. I thought that a touch greedy,' said Auntie.

'Nonsense, Amy, he's a charming boy.'

The crackers were pulled. 'I never imagined Mrs Cuthbert in a paper hat,' and Lottie giggled.

If Mr Soper were above himself, Auntie was out of herself and when they got up she clapped her hands. 'Come and sit down everybody and we'll have the presents.' She had found a pocket comb for Salvatore and wrapped it, as well as one of her father's lawn handkerchiefs for Mr Ruffino while for Violetta she opened the cabinet of her treasured possessions and sacrificed the miniature tea set which she swiftly packed in its box.

Lottie handed round the presents; there were cries of admiration and pleasure. 'You are clever, Lottie!' while Violetta had a little tea party for herself and Prince at once – a happy Violetta: there had not been a single puff of smoke or a 'No'.

'And now,' said Auntie when the wrappings and ribbons were all cleared away, 'Lottie is going to dance for us.'

'Not with Salvatore there I'm not.' Auntie had propelled Lottie into the bedroom to help her change. 'I won't.'

'Oh, come *on*.' Salvatore had followed them – he seemed to be everywhere. 'We're both first years . . . so you can't mind me.'

'I do mind you.'

'What are you going to *be*?' asked Salvatore.

'A Christmas fairy. Look how pretty,' said Auntie showing the tutu and wings. 'A very Christmas fairy.'

'I won't do it.'

'If I dance it with you it'll be lovely.' Salvatore was most coaxing. 'Come on. I'll be the Spirit of Christmas. My jersey's red. Have you any red tights?'

'Miss Dorcas and Miss Dora gave Lottie some for Christmas.'

'Fabulous! Miss Tew, can you make me a wreath with Lottie's red hairband and some bits of holly? Put glitter on my face. You do your dance, Charlotte, and I'll dance round you.'

'You'll spoil it.'

'I won't. I'll just fool.'

'And I'll run the tape a little longer,' said Auntie.

'You don't know the music.'

'Doesn't matter. I'll listen and at the end we'll join hands and spin round and round. Come on.'

The audience crowded against the walls and the furniture was moved back. Except for that morning of folk dancing, it was the first time Lottie had danced with Salvatore and she never forgot it. He did not get in her way but somersaulted and leapt round her. 'My word! That boy can leap,' said Mr Soper. Salvatore's body had the dexterity of an eel and to begin with he made Lottie's dancing look careful but soon she caught his exhilaration and what had been a pretty solo became a lively *pas de deux*.

Lottie had meant to end by touching everybody with her wand, which she did, but Salvatore took it from her, ran and put it by the Christmas tree, ran back and spun her round and round like a top then, taking her hands swung her round and round again till they fell gracefully on the floor. To the last chords they stood and did the *grande révérence*, two steps to the right, curtsy and bow, one to the left, bow and curtsy in a tumult of applause.

Afterwards they played games directed by Salvatore and Lottie. 'Why can't you always be nice like this?' she asked him.

'I really am nice most of the time,' said Salvatore. Lottie was almost ready to agree.

Quiet had fallen. Everyone was perhaps a little tired and Mr Ruffino began a carol. 'What a beautiful voice,' Mrs Cuthbert whispered to Auntie. It *was* beautiful, rich and mellow.

They all joined in until he sang alone: 'Silent night. Holy night ... '

Miss Dora began to weep a little – 'from happiness' she was to explain. Zanny, too, had tears in her eyes, perhaps thinking of her homeland; she held Emil's hand and, looking round the firelit room and its glistening tree, Lottie, kneeling on the hearthrug with Prince close asleep, thought how contented and peaceful everybody looked. Auntie had Violetta on her knee, leaning against her shoulder, the little girl's eyes full of sleep. Lottie saw Mr Ruffino looking at them. Even Salvatore, stretched out on the hearthrug too, still in his holly wreath which suited his dark hair, seemed to have no nastiness left in him.

It was when they were going home: Lottie had Prince in her arms ready to hand him over to Violetta. 'Keep him for the holidays,' suggested Mr Ruffino, but Lottie shook her head.

'I couldn't give him up all over again.' Salvatore came up to her.

'Prince is a pedigree puppy.'

'Yes,' said Lottie with pride. 'The vet told me.'

'My papa finds it very peculiar you found Prince in the street. I find it *very* peculiar too.'

Lottie looked at him with all her old dread and hate. 'Unpax,' she said.

'Very well, unpax. And you know what that means,' said Salvatore. 'War.'

# CHAPTER XI

The spring term began. To Lottie it was like coming home, Queen's Chase had become so dear and familiar. She was longing to tell about the party but Irene had gone from Switzerland to Australia, 'And my pony. In this horrible school you aren't allowed to ride, but I did,' said Irene.

'You can't ride and dance,' Priscilla pointed out. 'In riding your legs must turn in, in dancing, out. You can't do both.'

'I did.' Irene tossed her curls.

Priscilla told of Christmas in Nairobi, Anne-Marie of Delhi, while Sybil had had many parties, some of them in hotels, and happenings at Verbena Road sank into insignificance. It did not matter, there was dancing. 'My bones are getting better,' said Lottie.

For the first-year children, their second term was

quite different from their first. They were doing much the same things – 'Those dreary old *pliés* to begin with every time,' moaned Irene. 'All those exercises!' – but it was how they did them that was different. Lottie knew now she could trust her supporting leg to be strong, straight, knee firm unless she made a deliberate *fondu*; her instep was able now to hold a pointed foot; she could keep her back straight, head up, not letting her shoulders move and was able, without mystification, in the flick of a second, to follow Miss McKenzie's, Miss Hurley's, Mamzelly's, correcting voice: 'Down. Lift. Watch the back of that hand. Stretch. St-re-tch. Don't drop your hand, Irene.'

'Anne-Marie, *turn* your head.'

'Charlotte, your arms are a *little* too high.'

'Turn that leg out, OUT,' Miss Hurley would shout. 'Long waist. That's the way,' and, occasionally, mostly from Mamzelly, 'That's it. Good girls.'

They were, too, reunited with their prized *pointe* shoes and now it was not only the preparatory exercises. 'It's the beginning of real dancing,' said Lottie in bliss.

'Mr Ruffino is so kind,' said Auntie on the telephone. 'He says Sam goes to Queen's Chase on Saturday to fetch Salvatore and takes him back on Sunday evening. He has offered to take you too.' And before Lottie could speak, 'It would be lovely to have you on Saturday night. I wouldn't be so lonely.'

What could Lottie say to that? Not the 'I can't' that had been immediately ready.

'If Salvatore goes in front, I'll sit in the back,' said Lottie, but Sam looked at her.

'Salvatore won't bite you.'

How could Lottie say, in Salvatore's father's car, to Salvatore's chauffeur, 'I won't have anything to do with him'? It seemed, too, that she was tied to the Ruffinos. 'You'll meet us on the Heath and come to tea, won't you?' Sam pleaded. 'Vivi would be so happy.' When Lottie tried to hedge, 'She needs you,' said Sam. 'She hasn't many friends. Prince needs you too,' said Sam artfully. 'He's getting out of hand. He needs your training.'

Auntie, Violetta, Prince: more and more people seemed to need Lottie, and it was wonderful to be with Prince again, to hold his warm little body, feel his instant response. 'He's still your dog,' said Violetta which showed her sweetness. 'We'll have him together, Lottie.'

But each time Lottie saw him carried away in the big car with Violetta and Sam, 'I don't know how to bear it,' she told Auntie.

'Well, it's queer,' said Auntie, 'but it seems to me as if you are meant to go on seeing him. Perhaps it's the happiest thing under the circumstances.'

'Then I don't like the circumstances,' said Lottie.

It was not every Saturday. Irene asked Lottie for another weekend, 'Ma's set on having you ...'

Auntie demurred more strongly. 'It's our turn to ask Irene, but how can we?'

'You see,' Lottie told Mrs Challoner to whom she had gone in this dilemma, 'we've nothing to offer.' Auntie had said that.

'Nothing to offer! My dear child,' said Mrs Challoner, 'you and Auntie have something to offer that no one else can – at least not at Queen's Chase.'

Lottie was astounded. 'What?'

'Holbein's,' said Mrs Challoner. 'How many people who care about dancing, Mrs St Charles, for instance, or Priscilla's mother, have the chance to let their children go behind the scenes and see the workings of a famous little theatre and Company like Holbein's? Holbein's has become almost a legend. I hear Hilda Frost is having her first season and I'm sure if you asked her she would let you take Irene and Priscilla backstage. Your aunt would show them over the wardrobe – they could maybe watch a rehearsal. You say Hilda gives Auntie tickets, she might pass them on to you. Holbein's would be a rare part of ballet education, the parents would be so pleased.' Lottie was as dazzled as she was grateful.

'I never thought of that.'

'I can sleep on the sofa. Irene can have my bed,' she told Auntie.

'Blankets?' Auntie's voice rose.

'I'll bring my duvet from school.'

'Food?'

'We'll cook sausages, baked beans and scrambled egg. I've enough money saved to buy ice cream,' and at Auntie's look, 'That's the kind of food we like.'

'At Queen's Chase?' Auntie did not believe it. 'We must at least have a joint for Sunday.'

Irene seemed as enchanted by Holbein's as Lottie had hoped. She loved the little theatre, where Emil let them go into the box office, the orchestra pit, though she twanged the harp that stood ready for rehearsal. 'We *mustn't* do that,' said Lottie in trepidation. Emil took them on stage, and even let them climb the ladders up to the lights and flies. The scene was set for the opening of *Cat Among the Pigeons* and, 'What's that, Mr Emil?' Irene asked.

'It's the fountain in the convent garden,' said Lottie.

'You can turn it on if you like,' said Emil and, as the drops fell sparkling Lottie told her, "*Cat Among the Pigeons* was the first ballet Madame ever danced in, as the Humming Bird. There's a photograph of her in the foyer. Come and look.'

'Tonight we put a big basket of red roses in front of it,' said proud Emil and Irene was impressed.

Zanny pronounced her sweet while Auntie almost got over her fears. 'Such delightful manners. I think she really is enjoying herself,' she told Mrs Cuthbert.

But things began to perturb Lottie – Auntie too: the way Irene switched the television on without asking was not manners, particularly during meals which Auntie hated; the way Irene left most of her food untouched. On Saturday night, they were to go to the performance. 'Don't let's,' said Irene. 'Let's go to the cinema.'

'But Hilda has given us tickets.'

'We'll steal out. Nobody will notice.'

'They might,' but Irene prevailed as she always did with Lottie.

'If anyone does notice we'll say I didn't feel well and you had to take me home.'

It was perfectly plausible. 'But Hilda was hurt,' Auntie told them. 'She had planned a little supper party for you afterwards.'

'How were we to know?' Irene was belligerent.

'If you had been at the ballet, *which you had accepted*, you would have known,' said an unusually rebuking Auntie.

Irene was unrepentant. On Sunday morning when Auntie had gone, 'Does your aunt have to work on *Sundays?*' asked Irene.

'It's the Season.' Lottie had taken it for granted.

Then, 'Let's go and see Salvatore,' said Irene.

'*Salvatore?*' Lottie was astounded. 'I thought you detested Salvatore?'

'I do, but at least he's not boring,' which meant, Lottie knew, that Verbena Road was boring. All the same she flatly refused.

'My dears, you should have seen it,' said Irene as her mother often said. 'To begin with they live in a basement.'

It was the free time before afternoon lessons began but Lottie was on her way to the extra coaching in mathematics she needed – she was trying hard to catch up. As she crossed the lower hall she saw that a knot of girls was gathered round Irene. They were so avid that they did not see Lottie.

'Fusty old red curtains they're so proud of because they belonged to their precious Madame. Charlotte had to sleep on the sofa in the sitting room because I had her bed. She seemed to do most of the cooking.'

'Heavens! What was it like?'

'Nursery food!' Lottie thought of the joint of lamb that had seemed so extravagant to her and Auntie.

'And it was Holbein's, Holbein's all the time. They went on and on about it.'

'They say it's going to fail,' said Pamela. 'The Company isn't any good now.'

'You'd think it was the stars and that aunt of hers kept flapping. "Are you all right, dear?" "Dearie, have you had enough?" "Dearie, have some more of our disgusting ice-cream."' Irene mimicked Auntie to perfection and Lottie burned for her.

'Sounds pretty miz to me,' said Anne-Marie.

'It was. I thought it was never going to end!'

Charlotte left her books and fled up to the dormitory; they were not allowed there in the daytime but she did not care. She sat on her bed numb with shock and shame for Auntie and for herself. Then, How, *how*, she wondered, can I ever see Irene again?

That was the beginning of disenchantment and real trouble for Lottie at Queen's Chase.

'Charlotte, I want to talk to you.'

'Well, I don't want to talk to you.'

'You had better for your own good.' Salvatore said it like an old schoolmaster. He had cornered Lottie in the orangery museum where she had gone to take notes for a project.

'How could *you* talk to me for my own good?' she sneered.

'You'll see.' Salvatore had her cornered against the

plinth of the statue of the girl in a metallic tutu. He was bubbling with pleasure.

'I told you, my papa thinks it *most* peculiar that you found a valuable little dog in the street. So did I – until I knew you didn't.' Lottie's heart gave a sickening thump. 'There was a pet shop, wasn't there?'

'How do you know?' Lottie whispered it.

'Somebody told me.'

'They couldn't have. I never told anyone, not even Auntie.' Then remembrance came back. 'Except . . .' But she wouldn't. She couldn't, was Lottie's quick thought. Didn't she say, 'May I die if I lie'? 'Irene wouldn't,' she said aloud.

'She did.' Salvatore chortled with glee and Lottie knew it was true that if Irene thought someone did not like her – Salvatore had detested her – she went out of her way to win them. She could have done nothing that pleased Salvatore more because now Lottie would have to, 'Do what I want,' said Salvatore. 'I like making people do what I want, especially girls. Especially you.'

'Why me?'

'Because you won't have anything to do with me,' said Salvatore plainly. 'Now you'll have to.'

'I won't.'

'I think you will. You *were* silly. If you had to tell

someone why didn't you tell me? I wouldn't have told, not ever.'

Oddly enough, Lottie believed him.

'I wouldn't have told, but now . . . '

'Now?' quavered Lottie.

He came close. 'You stole Prince. You knew he came from the pet shop. You should have taken him back but you kept him. That's stealing. If Mrs Challoner knew, she'd have to tell the governors and they wouldn't keep you. They might tell the police. You could be sent to *prison*,' cried Salvatore, his eyes bright.

'They don't send children to prison.' Lottie held on to the remnant of her sense and gathered herself to say, 'If you want to know I'm saving up all my money to go to that shop to pay for Prince.'

'Hoo! Hoo!' Salvatore collapsed in laughter. 'You haven't any money.' He seemed to fathom that she was at present saving for Auntie's birthday gloves. I have to do that first, then I'll start for Prince, but Salvatore was saying: 'You may not go to prison but they won't keep you at Queen's Chase because it's my duty to tell.'

'You'll tell?'

'Yes. Unless . . . '

'Unless?'

'You do exactly what I say.'

'What sort of things?' asked Lottie cautiously.

'I'll think of them. I've always wanted a genie,' and Salvatore was not altogether teasing. 'I'll be the magician who has the magic ring – you'll be the genie.'

'What's a genie?'

'The slave of the ring. When I rub it you'll appear.'

'What if I won't?'

'You know what,' said Salvatore.

Since the time Lottie had heard Irene telling about Verbena Road – and she had an extra reason now with the broken promise – the more Lottie tried to avoid her the more Irene seemed to want to be with her. Lottie did not want even to speak to Irene, she was too sick and sore at heart and when, after supper one evening Irene came to her and whispered, 'Ssh! The Salon's empty. Let's take our *pointe* shoes and practise there', Lottie should have turned her back, at least said, 'I won't practise anything with you.'

Instead, feeble as it was, 'We're not allowed,' she said.

'Pooh!'

'Irene, we're not allowed to touch our *pointe* shoes out of class, not even take them home.'

'Well, I've brought yours and mine. You can do a little *barre* work as you're so afraid. I'm going to dance.'

Mamzelly found them, '*Grand Dieu!*' screamed Mamzelly. '*Quelle sottise!* Undo those ribbons at once.

163

Give me those shoes. You will not have them back for a fortnight. Every time we do *pointe* work you will sit like two dunces on two chairs. You naughty ...' Mamzelly made it sound like 'notty', 'notty little girls.'

'I'm sorry, Mamzelly,' Irene was unaccustomedly meek, 'but Charlotte thought it would be fun.'

*Charlotte* thought! Lottie gasped but Mamzelly turned on her. 'You are supposed to be a sensible girl. Give me those shoes,' and with the shoes she stalked off.

'She'll tell Miss McKenzie,' said Irene. 'Charlotte, I'm sorry I had to say it was you but it's very important I shouldn't get into trouble just now. I'll tell you what none of the others know about yet. Geoffrey Pick, the choreographer, is doing a ballet for the Company this summer, *The Birthday of the Infanta.* As it's about children, some of you will be in it but I'm to be the little Infanta.'

Little Infanta or not, Lottie looked at Irene not in admiration but disgust.


'You will spend this week's pocket money on sweets and give them all to me,' ordered Salvatore.

'I can't. I'm saving up for gloves for Auntie's birthday.'

'Poor Auntie.'

Lottie had tried to find out what Salvatore would make her do as a genie. 'Not anything I shouldn't,' she pleaded.

'Maybe,' said Salvatore and sure enough, 'You'll get up

in the middle of the night and meet me for a midnight feast in the museum. You'll bring the feast.'

'How can I?'

'Steal apples. You're good at stealing,' said this cruel Salvatore. 'Besides it's easy.' Apples were put on the tables in bowls. 'Encourage us to eat fruit,' mocked Salvatore. 'I'll bring some things from home. Before you go to bed at nine o'clock go into the office – Daphne will have gone home – and open the window just a crack. In the boys' wing there's the top of a lavatory window left open at night. I can wriggle through and come round outside. We'll meet at midnight.'

'I'll never wake.'

'I'll come and wake you. Then I'd like you to go walking by yourself in the Park.'

'It's out of bounds.'

'That's why. Then food. I'm very fond of food.'

'So am I.' Lottie tried to put up a defence.

'At mealtimes you'll bring your tray next to mine. I'll tell you what to choose. Ask the counter ladies for a large helping. I'll take half. Same with seconds.'

'I don't have second helpings.'

'You will now.'

'They'll notice.'

'Not they,' which again was true; serving more than a hundred hungry children, the counter ladies had no time to notice – besides, Salvatore was a born thief, so adroit that he had taken half of Lottie's dinner before she noticed.

She noticed afterwards. 'Salvatore, I'm hungry.'

'Good,' said Salvatore.

What Irene had told Lottie was true and soon a rumour was running through the school; there was to be a new ballet and some of the children would be in it. 'Even the first years?'

'Particularly the first years.'

Then Miss McKenzie confirmed it: a new ballet choreographed by Geoffrey Pick, the Company's young choreographer. 'He was here as a boy. We used to call him Pickles,' and, 'Yes, the ballet concerns you, some of you. It is called *The Birthday of the Infanta* from a famous story, not a children's story though it is about children. The Infanta is ten years old. Mr Pick will choose his dancers soon.'

Miss Hurley told them about it in her History of Ballet class: '*Infanta* is the Spanish for princess, so the ballet is set in Spain but not at all the Spain most of us think of for Spanish dancing, flounced skirts, mantillas with high combs, stamping heels, castanets clicking. This is the Spanish court in the time of Philip IV, seventeenth century, and will be designed after Velázquez the great

166

Spanish court painter,' and Miss Hurley showed them a print of the wonderful painting, *Las Meniñas*, which shows the little Infanta in her stiff parchment-coloured dress, a rose in her hair, with her ladies-in-waiting and attended by dwarfs and a great dog.

There was a murmur. 'She looks like Irene. Of course, Irene will be the Infanta.'

'Of course,' said Irene.

They looked for a long time at the painting. '*Las Meniñas* means the ladies-in-waiting,' said Miss Hurley. In their farthingaled brown and black dresses they were vying for the little princess's attention; the painter had put himself into the painting, standing at his easel, but, 'Why dwarfs?' asked the children.

'Dwarfs were supposed to be amusing then.'

The ballet was about a dwarf and Miss Hurley told the poignant story of the boy dwarf who had lived in the forest all his life and seen no other people but his father, a woodcutter, until one day when he was playing with the forest butterflies, the King's huntsman saw him and bought him from the woodcutter as a present for the Infanta Margarita, on her tenth birthday.

She and other young noble boys and girls, princes, dukes, counts and little duchesses and countesses came to the palace gardens for an entertainment. There were gypsies who sang, performing monkeys, a man with a bear, a mock bullfight which the noble boys fought, the toreadors on hobby horses richly caparisoned and at the end, the dwarf was brought on in a cage. Lottie could never bear that moment in the ballet – 'A cage!'

The dwarf was to be danced by Shaun Donaghue, short enough to be a dwarf on stage and not only a fine dancer but a natural actor; it was for him that Geoffrey Pick had created the ballet. When the dwarf was let out of his cage, dressed up in court finery, the children clapped and shouted with laughter, even the Infanta. Dwarfs or anyone misshapen or idiot seemed wonderfully funny to the court but the dwarf mistook the applause for admiration and danced and anticked with delight. The Infanta gave him a ring from her finger, which one of the courtiers pocketed immediately. Then she gave the dwarf the rose from her hair. He went down on one knee to receive it and kissed her little white hand. The children shouted with laughter but in his simple mind, She loves me, he had thought. Why else did she give me her ring? You must remember the only place he had seen his face and poor body was in a pool in the forest and there the wind made ripples and he could not see clearly. How could he know how hideous he was? How different from the noble young bullfighters though he too had been dressed up.

It was time for the banquet. The Infanta led the way into the palace; the dwarf was left alone in the garden.

But she'll come back to me, he thought. She loves me. The flowers in the garden tried to warn him; the roses, lilies, geraniums and cacti – this was a pretty part of the ballet. His friends the butterflies tried to tell him but could not remember what they had to say; the nightingale sang a lament.

At last he found his way into the palace, into the throne room which was empty. Carried away he sat on the throne, then danced to where a velvet curtain hung; he drew it aside and there was a great mirror. At once he saw he was not alone. Facing him was a figure, a monster, hunchbacked – malformed. He moved, it moved. He knelt, it knelt. He put his face against the mirror, it came to meet him. At last he knew it was himself. With a cry he fell to the ground racked with sobs.

The Infanta and her guests came back and looked at him, puzzled by the sobbing. 'Your dancing was good,' she said. 'Your acting is better, but now you must get up and dance for me.'

The dwarf had stopped sobbing and was still.

'Yes,' all the children cried. 'Get up.' But the little dwarf made no answer.

The Infanta stamped her foot and sent for the Court Chamberlain. 'My funny little dwarf is sulking. Tell him to get up and dance.'

The Chamberlain bent over him, then stood up. 'Mi

bella Princesa, my beautiful Princess, your little dwarf will never dance again.'

'But why will he not dance again?' asked the Infanta laughing.

'Because his heart is broken,' answered the Chamberlain.

The Infanta frowned. 'For the future,' she said, 'let those who come to play with me have no hearts,' and danced away into the garden.

Lottie was moved to tears. 'How I would like to dance in that ballet.'

Irene tried to make amends. 'Ma wants you to come for the weekend. She has tickets for a musical. It would be fun. Ask your auntie, will you, and come.'

'No, thank you.' Lottie had pleasure in saying it.

'Why not?' Irene challenged her.

'Because' – Lottie heard again those voices in the hall – 'because you don't live in a basement or do the cooking and have nursery food.' She was trembling. 'Because your ma might ask me to have some more disgusting ice cream. Because *I* might think it was never going to end.'

Irene had the grace to blush. 'You can't believe what you hear . . . ' she began.

'I do believe what I hear when somebody says it, so I wouldn't *dream* of coming to you for the weekend.'

\*

Mr Pickles, as the children called him, came to watch them in class and soon it was confirmed that Irene was to dance the Infanta which made her plume. Salvatore was to be her partner, the noble young Don Alfonso, boy Duke of Toledo. Twenty other boys and girls were chosen from the first and second years including Sybil, Anne-Marie, Desmond and little Thomas. 'I suggested you,' Miss McKenzie told Lottie, 'but lately your dancing has fallen off. Why? Charlotte, is something wrong?'

'Yes.' Lottie wanted to cry but instead had to say, 'Nothing that I can't manage.'

That nettled Miss McKenzie. 'I wasn't going to tell you, Charlotte, what Mr Pick said about your dancing but I think I will. "There's no zing in it," which means no life.'

Zing. The word stung.

# CHAPTER XII

Lottie had no pocket money left; she had given it all to Salvatore – Auntie's gloves had receded into the distance. Lottie had gone for the prescribed walks until a keeper stopped her. 'He said, "Little lady,"' she told Salvatore, '"in February the stags are rutting which means they fight. It's dangerous to go off the paths."'

To her surprise Salvatore was angry – not because she could not walk but because she had walked. 'Who told you to go near the stags?' he ranted. 'You're not to go out again, do you hear? If you do I'll tell everyone everything at once.'

They did have one midnight feast, and Lottie had to admit it was thrilling, partly from the fear of being caught though Salvatore taught her how to be quiet as a mouse.

She had managed to creep into the office and unlatch the window. At midnight Salvatore had come silently to wake her, putting one hand over her mouth which gave her a terrible start – his hand was deadly cold – but stifled any sound. 'Ssh! Come on,' he mouthed in her ear and leaving a pillow for a shape in her bed and taking her apples they crept downstairs by the glimmer of a pocket torch he kept in his hand. Once in the museum they could relax, it was away from the house, and he set out a real picnic behind a showcase. He had a small sack, 'Like a burglar,' he whispered, pushing it ahead of him through the lavatory and study windows, and had brought cold sausages, delicious biscuits, crisps, chocolate bars and a bottle of Coke. He had remembered the opener and even brought a box of matches and a nightlight which shed a warm little light on it all.

It turned out a real feast. There was plenty for both of them, Lottie could eat as much as she liked and Salvatore was as he had been at Christmas and even more funny. He did a sketch of Mr Ormond walking through the school finding fault. 'Ssh, Lottie, you're laughing out loud,' and of Miss McKenzie in class, 'Thomas, keep your tail in. Boys, do you *ever* keep still? Go and do twenty fast jumps at the *barre*.' Salvatore did twenty without any *barre*.

They jumped themselves when the big clock in the hall struck one. Salvatore slid out of the office window – Lottie did not envy him going round outside in the dark.

She closed the window noiselessly and, guided by the banisters, made her way up the staircase and found herself breathless with excitement in her bed, too excited to sleep.

It was the only time. 'Where were you?' Salvatore stormed. 'I came and the window was shut.'

'I tried two or three times but Mrs Gillespie was there telephoning and then Mrs Challoner and they stayed talking,' and she rebelled. 'I can't open the office window any more.'

'Not to worry,' said Salvatore and came closer. 'At night,' he said, 'I can come through doors without opening them.'

Lottie should have said, 'Get away!' but in her wrought-up state she half believed he would appear by her bed and lay awake dreading the moment when that small cold hand would cover her mouth. Salvatore never appeared, it was empty boasting, but by then, in any case, she was too hungry to sleep. She heard the clock strike eleven, twelve, one, then fell into such a deep sleep she did not hear the bell. Priscilla, who slept next to her, had to shake her awake and then Lottie almost fell asleep at breakfast.

At first Salvatore had taken one rasher of bacon, a piece of fried bread, a part of her meat, only two potatoes but soon, 'I was overcome by greed,' he was to tell Mrs

Challoner. 'That's practically all my ice-cream,' protested Lottie. She loved cheese toast. 'You've taken it *all*!'

'You can eat the tomato,' said Salvatore.

'You've taken all the ham and left me the salad. What'll the girls think?' she challenged him.

'Tell them you've turned vegetarian.'

Lottie was still at Irene's table though she would rather not have been. 'Trying to get thin, Charlotte?' Irene scoffed. 'You're like a bean pole already.'

In February, too, it snowed: the pond was frozen, the trees white with rime-frost. The colours of the deer seemed deeper against the snow in the park. In the day-time the sky was clear but in the early sunset took on a pearly pink as did the snow. It was beautiful but for Lottie the cold made her hunger worse. Food! Food! Food was what she mostly thought of. Mrs Challoner let the whole school go sledging, the younger children made snowmen but Lottie did not feel like playing or running and stood about getting colder so that her hunger gnawed.

She had a respite from Salvatore at weekends and had counted on half-term. 'Have a good rest,' said Miss McKenzie. 'You've been looking very tired lately,' but there was no rest.

Auntie too said, 'You're looking what I call peaky. Are they working you too hard?'

'Of course not.'

'Well, you stay quiet here.' But there was no quiet either; Auntie had not finished her breakfast before Mr Soper called her to the telephone. It was Hilda; Lottie, who had followed Auntie, heard her peremptory voice. 'Oh dear!' said Auntie when she came back. 'Another dress to alter. You'll have to go to the bead shop for me, dearie. I shall need more gauze and sequins. Never mind, Sunday's coming. We'll have a nice chicken,' but Auntie had to work on Sunday and there was no chicken.

All this was because Hilda's second Season at Holbein's was opening after Easter and she was having trouble. 'She doesn't seem able to keep her dancers or hold the Company together,' said Auntie deeply worried. 'Perhaps because she takes so many of the chief roles herself.' Two girls had stormed out in the middle of rehearsal and each time it meant costume alterations or fresh ones. Lottie was kept busy going down to the West End to match patterns, or to the bead shop or tacking hems for Auntie or ironing. There was, too, little time for cooking – she had meant to cook and cook – and there was little to cook with. She came back to Queen's Chase even more tired and then, surprisingly, she did not want to eat. It was Priscilla who said, 'You're being very silly, Charlotte. We're supposed to eat. You only had cereal and toast for breakfast. How can you dance? You can't.'

'No zing.' Try as she might, Lottie could not get any zing; it seemed to have gone out of her as well as her dancing and soon it was like the time with Hilda, in Prince's early days.

'That's a feeble attempt from you at *grands battements*,' scolded Miss Hurley.

'Charlotte. I have spoken to you *twice*! I shall not speak again.' That was Mamzelly.

Worst of all was Miss McKenzie. 'If that's the best you can do, you'd better sit down. I'll see you after class.'

Miss McKenzie tried again. 'You can't be well.'

'I am well, honest.'

'Then I must remind you that assessment isn't far off.' Assessment was when the governors came to Queen's Chase and, with the staff, assessed every boy and girl to see how they were progressing and, 'Don't tell me, Charlotte, that you're going to fail assessment.' Charlotte looked at Miss McKenzie in desperation. 'Let's see if you can't pull yourself together and try harder.' She had no idea how hard Lottie was trying already but next lesson when, 'From the corner,' called Miss McKenzie. 'One by one, polka *en diagonale*. Now, right foot pointed, step on to three-quarter *pointe* with right foot, close left foot behind in fifth position, step with right foot on to flat foot and hop passing left leg with a small *developpé* pointing to the floor. Repeat, three springs, *pointes* changing, left, right, left to the front. Close both feet together with a jump.'

Lottie made a tremendous effort and started off with a zing and, 'Good girl,' said Miss McKenzie but when it came to the repeat, the studio suddenly began to whirl round Lottie; she stood, swayed and fell *flump* on the floor.

'Charlotte?' Irene was across the room as Jonah Templeton, the pianist, stopped the music abruptly. The other girls would have followed but, 'Stay back, all of you,' ordered Miss McKenzie. By the calmness of her voice girls might have fainted in her class every day. 'Leave this to Jonah and me.' That she said Jonah instead of Mr Templeton showed that, really, she was shocked. 'That's right, Irene.' Irene had pillowed Lottie's head on her knee and was rubbing her hands; Priscilla who, in spite of Miss McKenzie, had followed, rubbed Lottie's legs; the rest of the girls stood awed, Sybil sobbing. 'I'll just ask the office to tell Sister . . . ' Miss McKenzie spoke on the intercom. 'Now, Jonah, if we—'

'I can take her.' Jonah lifted Lottie from the ground. 'Irene, get my coat and put it over her. Jean,' he spoke to Miss McKenzie, 'if you would open the door.'

'Don't stand about and get cold,' Miss McKenzie ordered again. 'Go on with your exercises at the *barre*.

Priscilla, you lead. I won't be more than a few minutes. Sybil, if you haven't got a handkerchief get a Kleenex from the changing room.'

'Mrs Challoner! Mrs Challoner!' The piercing cry filled the hall as, ducking past Daphne in the office outside, Salvatore burst into the Yellow Drawing Room. 'Mrs Challoner!'

'Salvatore! Do you have to come in like a tornado?' Then seeing his stricken face, 'What *is* the matter?' asked Mrs Challoner.

'Matter! I think I may have killed Charlotte Tew.'

He had been crossing the hall with the other boys, going from a history lesson to change for dancing, when they met the small procession. 'Quiet, boys,' Miss McKenzie had said. 'There's been an accident.'

They had stood in awe but Salvatore had let out a howl and fled to the Yellow Drawing Room, where he flung himself on Mrs Challoner. 'Jonah was carrying her. She had been dancing. She was covered with his coat. One arm hung down. She was all white. Oh what have I done? What *have* I done?'

'If you will let me stand up,' said Mrs Challoner, 'I'll go and see what you have done. You stay here till I come back.'

*

'Absolutely nothing wrong.' Dr Paul put away his stethoscope. 'Everything is normal except', he looked again at Lottie who had been put to bed in the infirmary, 'except she's very weak.'

'Weak? One of *ours*?' Sister was incredulous.

'That's what I find surprising. One of yours. They injure themselves—'

'Often,' said Sister with feeling.

'Get colds, flu, usual things like tonsillitis and mumps but this child seems ... debilitated.'

'She can't be.'

'Is she likely to have fads, like getting slim though there's almost nothing to slim? Does she eat enough?'

'Mrs Robinson who helps me here' – Sister nodded towards a plump cheerful woman who was folding up Lottie's clothes – 'is one of our canteen ladies and does the serving. She'll tell you how they eat.'

'Charlotte has always eaten well,' said Mrs Robinson, 'and lately she's been having second helpings.'

'She has always been an unusually sensible child,' Sister endorsed.

'Does she come from a poor or careless home?'

'Not exactly poor, besides you know how we treat our children ...'

'Tie them up when they're not dancing, beat them and starve them,' Dr Paul teased, then, 'Seriously, Sister.'

'It's a mystery,' said Sister when Dr Paul had gone.

'No it isn't,' said Mrs Challoner coming in. 'I have just had a complete and theatrical confession from Master Salvatore Ruffino.'

'It was like a snowball rolling in snow,' Salvatore had told her, looking out of the window at the snow. 'It gets so big you can't stop it.' It was then he said, 'I suppose I was overcome by greed.'

'You certainly were,' said Mrs Challoner.

'Charlotte's always so serious and so good and it was such fun.'

'It wasn't,' said Mrs Challoner. 'It never is when the magician forgets about the poor genie. Fortunately I don't think you have damaged Charlotte irreparably but it might have been serious for her and this will have to go to Miss Glyn and the governors.'

'Oh no! Not *again*. Put me on bread and water,' he begged.

'Bread and water won't meet the case. You will probably lose your dancing – we can't tolerate bullies.'

'Me – a bully!' Salvatore was shocked.

'Yes. The only mitigating thing is that you came to me and told me. Tell me one thing more. What was it that gave you such a hold on Charlotte that she could not tell anyone?'

'I can't tell either,' said Salvatore. 'I promised.'

'I thought that honourable,' Mrs Challoner told the governors.

'So do I,' said Polly who had been questioned about Salvatore's route through the lavatory window. ('I wouldn't have believed even a small boy could get through it.') 'Honourable, particularly when he was hoping to be let off.'

'Surely now he must be expelled,' said Mr Ormond.

'Never!' Miss McKenzie was in trepidation. 'They couldn't think of it with *The Birthday of the Infanta* so near?'

Salvatore was suspended for the rest of the term with the proviso that he must attend rehearsals. Mr Ruffino was sent for to take him away.

'Charlotte, Salvatore is asking to see you.'

Lottie had been kept in bed all day and lay with what would have been an enormous feeling of relief if she had not had an equally enormous apprehension: only Salvatore could dispel that and, to Mrs Challoner's surprise, she said, 'Yes please.' The moment he appeared she reared herself up in bed. 'You've told.'

'Am I Irene? What do you think?'

'You mean you didn't tell?'

'Of *course* not. Only what I did to you.'

'That was good of you, Salvatore.' Lottie had to say it.

'Yes, it was but, Lottie—'

'Who said you could call me Lottie?'

'I did at the midnight feast. Look, here's your pocket money back, all that you spent for me on sweets, and I've made mine match it.' He put down quite a wad of notes on the bed.

'I don't want your money.'

'You do because you know what?'

'What?'

'It's quite a lot of money so now you can go to the pet shop and pay for Prince.'

'Pay – for – Prince? *Now?*' Lottie felt she might faint again.

'Yes. You hadn't thought of that, had you? Then it won't matter who tells. You can tell everyone and everyone will admire you. I think it's brilliant.'

It was but Lottie quailed at the thought of going to the pet shop.

'Prince is my concern now as well as yours,' Salvatore was arguing. 'I'm Violetta's brother so *I'll* come with you.'

It was a way out: for Lottie it was as if a ray of light had broken through her darkness. It would take Salvatore to think of it, was her instinctive thought but there was something bragging and proprietorial in the way he said, 'I'll come with you' that made her say at once, 'I wouldn't go anywhere with you.'

'Go by yourself, then,' said Salvatore, and shrugged.

Go by yourself. I can't, thought Lottie in bed. They wouldn't believe me – or Salvatore – we're children. But who could she ask? Auntie? She could well imagine the fuss Auntie would get into, the dismay – and reproach. 'Oh, Lottie. You should have told me. I would never have let you keep Prince.' But I kept him, thought Lottie in rebellion. Mrs Challoner? She might still send me away. Lion? Lion was still abroad. He had not come for Hilda's Season. 'The rat!' Auntie had said, which had surprised Lottie almost out of her skin: she had never heard Auntie use a word like that.

Mr Soper? Somehow even Lottie knew Mr Soper was not suitable but, I must be quick, thought Lottie, because any moment Irene might tell – she may have told already but then surely someone would have said. If Lottie had only known, Irene had almost forgotten about her: she had never been interested in Prince and was far too taken up with being Irene really to bother with anyone else, particularly this new Irene who was to be the little Infanta and was having private rehearsals with Mr Pick. 'It doesn't seem to be doing your dancing any good,' Miss Hurley warned her, but Irene did not even take offence. 'Soon I'm to be measured for my dress,' she said as if she had not heard.

Lying in bed, supposed to be resting, Lottie tossed and

turned. Then Sister came in. 'You seem to be holding quite a *levée*,' said Sister.

'What's a *levée*?'

'When the king or queen used to receive visitors as they got up or even in bed. Here's Salvatore's papa, Mr Ruffino, to see you. What a fuss about a little girl!'

Mr Ruffino could not contain himself. 'What can I say to you?' he asked Lottie. 'I could not believe my ears!' and he said what he had said before. 'My Salvatore to do such things! This time I shall beat him – mercilessly.'

'No, oh no!' cried Lottie. 'Please don't beat him, Mr Ruffino,' but he was going on.

'You of all little girls! I have such regard for your aunt. I shall have to call on her immediately. Salvatore shall come too and make apology but no apology can mend this and you, poor little miss. What can I do for you? Get for you? Anything. *Anything*,' declared Mr Ruffino.

Lottie suddenly made up her mind. 'There is one thing,' she said. 'Mr Ruffino, I need a grown-up.'

'You mean to tell me', said Mr Ruffino when Lottie had finished, 'that our little dog Prince was stolen?'

'I'm afraid so,' said Lottie in misery.

'And you were part of it?' Again Mr Ruffino passed his folded handkerchief over his forehead as if he were bewildered.

'I didn't exactly steal – the big boy did that. I – I just didn't give Prince back. Oh, I know,' said Lottie, 'I ought to have. I've thought about it all these nights, but now Salvatore says I can pay for Prince.'

'*Salvatore* says?'

'Yes, with my pocket money and his. It's funny he helps me as well as—'

'Tormenting,' Mr Ruffino finished for her, but his face had lightened. 'He's not all bad, that one.'

'Yes. Mr Ruffino will you come with me to the pet shop soon?'

'We'll go tomorrow.'

'But nobody must know.' Lottie was still anxious. 'Not even Auntie until it's all over. They're sending me home for the weekend tomorrow, so I thought . . .'

'I will fetch you,' said Mr Ruffino. 'Tomorrow is Friday. They will think I am delivering you home – it is the least that I can do – but we'll make a little excursion, you and I.'

'Just us,' pleaded Lottie. 'Not Salvatore.'

'We will leave Mr Salvatore at home.' Mr Ruffino chuckled. 'Serve him right. He likes to have a finger in every pie. In any case he is banished for the rest of term except for these so important rehearsals. Tomorrow afternoon then, you and I.'

\*

'Well I never!' said the pet-shop lady. She was wearing what might have been the same pink overall. 'They didn't catch the boy, though I called the police, and I have worried and worried about that puppy. You ought—' she began severely to Lottie, but Mr Ruffino intervened.

'Miss Charlotte knows that, which is why we are here. Prince – we call the puppy Prince . . . '

'A good name for him.'

'Yes. He has a good home with us and she has saved to pay you for him.'

'We've saved twelve pounds,' said Lottie proudly.

'That ought to do it,' Salvatore had said. Salvatore who, she thought, knew everything, but the pet-shop lady began to laugh.

'My dear little girl! For that puppy we were asking a hundred and twenty pounds.'

If the shop floor had risen up and hit Lottie she could not have been more stunned. 'A hundred – and – twenty pounds for a little puppy – but he was only this big.' She showed with her hands.

'A hundred and twenty pounds is the price of a pure-bred pedigree Cavalier King Charles spaniel nowadays.'

'Then . . . we'll have to bring him back.'

All Lottie's new and hopeful world had tumbled, but again Mr Ruffino spoke. 'This, Madam, is precisely why I came. I had foreseen. Yes, Charlotte, I had foreseen. And do you think I would let my Violetta be parted from Prince? You will pay the lady your twelve pounds, for the rest I shall make you a loan.'

'But, Mr Ruffino, I can never ever pay you back.'

'You can pay me back', said Mr Ruffino, 'when you are a *ballerina assoluta*,' and reserved quiet Lottie threw her arms round Mr Ruffino and hugged him.

'I don't know what to say,' said Auntie when Mr Ruffino brought Lottie home.

'Say nothing,' he urged her. 'Isn't it all done and past?' but Auntie was not to be put off as easily.

'To think how carefully I brought you up,' she reproached Lottie. 'If I had known, you would have taken Prince back *at once*. And not only that,' said Auntie. 'All this time you have been deceiving me. Oh, Lottie! I wouldn't have thought it of you, I wouldn't have believed it. I ought to punish you severely.'

Lottie stood shamed and silent but Mr Ruffino put his arm round her. 'Dear Miss Tew,' he said. 'Do you not think Charlotte has been punished enough? She has suffered a great deal for that little dog. Can you not forgive her and let him be? He is happy and well. We should all be so happy, Miss Tew.'

Auntie could not resist that. 'But the money, Mr Ruffino. How can I let you spend all that?'

'It is for Violetta ... to lose Prince would break her little heart. Besides, Charlotte is going to repay me.'

'When I'm a principal,' said Lottie.

It ended by Mr Ruffino's staying to drink what was left of Mr Soper's sherry and Lottie having the longest and most peaceful night's sleep she had had for weeks.

For Auntie there was only now one worry. 'I dread to think what Edna Cuthbert will say about this.'

'She can't say anything if you don't tell her,' said Lottie. 'The only grown-ups who have to know are you and Mr Ruffino and yes, I think Mrs Challoner.'

'Well, you were a little silly,' said Mrs Challoner. 'If you had thought, you would have known that Salvatore would never do anything that would upset Violetta. He would never have told about Prince. He wouldn't even tell me,' and, 'If you want to stay at Queen's Chase, Charlotte, you must use your common sense.'

Miss McKenzie, though she did not know about Prince – and did not ask – was the worst.

'I didn't mean to hurt my dancing,' Lottie told her when, on Monday, she came early to Miss McKenzie's class to say sorry.

'Then you weren't thinking. Why is there a rule that if you don't eat at least two courses at breakfast you cannot dance that day? A rule you broke – or you let Salvatore make you break. Don't you know that everything you do, everything that happens to you, affects your dancing?' and Lottie remembered how, long ago – it seemed very long ago – Madame had sent her out of her class because she had dirty finger-nails.

'I don't see what finger-nails have to do with dancing,' Lottie had dared to say when Madame spoke to her afterwards.

'Then you are a block,' and Madame had said much like Miss McKenzie, 'All of you, every little bit is to do with your dancing.'

Lottie had thought that was going too far but, as if she had said that aloud, 'Nor nearly far enough,' said Madame. 'For you, everything you see and hear and touch, taste and smell is to do with dancing, *if* you are a dancer.'

Now, 'You are here at Queen's Chase to dance,' said Miss McKenzie sternly. 'Don't forget that.' Then she relented. 'And you *can* dance. Never forget that either.' She gave a deep sigh. 'Oh, Charlotte, I can't help saying how much I wish you were in *The Birthday of the Infanta*.'

# CHAPTER XIII

Lottie knew all about the ballet. 'Anyone who is any-where near Irene cannot help knowing,' as Angela said.

'I am the youngest child who has ever taken the chief part in a major ballet,' Irene preened. 'After all Clara in *The Nutcracker* is usually twelve. I shall be in all the news-papers, you'll see.' And she would say, 'I mustn't do this – or that – in case I get tired.'

'It isn't doing your dancing any good.' Miss Hurley had said it before and it was true. Irene hardly paid any atten-tion in class. Yet Lottie noticed, to her surprise, neither Miss Hurley nor Mamzelly, not even Miss McKenzie, found fault with her; they let her be, and Lottie remem-bered what Hilda had told her of teachers, 'The better they think you are the more they criticise.' But surely, thought Lottie, to be chosen as the Infanta must mean that Irene's the best child dancer at Queen's Chase?

Now, 'Jean, Jean.' A voice was calling and there was a

rush of steps as Geoffrey Pick came tearing into the studio. 'Jean. I've got the monkeys.'

'Monkeys?'

'For the ballet.' To Geoffrey Pick there was only one ballet in the world, his *Birthday of the Infanta*. 'They should have been Barbary apes, according to the story, but those are so hideous. These are perfect. Come and see.'

'I have a class, Pickles. I'll be an hour.'

'Bother your class. Come and see and call the boys,' but Pickles had to wait.

Miss McKenzie loved the theatre even more than she loved the classroom and was already immersed in rehearsing the children chosen for *The Birthday of the Infanta*.

The smaller girls and boys were to be noble children or pages; they had to learn to pace, walk, sometimes backwards, curtsy and bow, but the highlight for Miss McKenzie was the pavane, a stately court dance for Irene and Salvatore before the entertainment began, she in her Velázquez dress of stiff parchment-coloured silk, a rose in her hair, he the boy Duke of Toledo in court dress, full velvet pantaloons and doublet, gold-laced, sleeves of palest silk, short satin cloak and shoulder sash of honour, silk hose and velvet shoes, a stiff white ruff setting off his hair which was to be cut with a fringe. 'Like a girl,' said the boys in derision – all the boys in the ballet had been told to let their hair grow – 'And we have to wear lace!'

Desmond said in disgust, he was Prince Baltasar Carlos, the Infanta's brother.

Salvatore did not mind at all, he gloried in his costume and, 'That boy has panache,' said Pickles. 'He'll bring the house down.'

'Yes. It's a good thing Irene's so pretty,' said Miss McKenzie.

When the pavane was over the Infanta was led, as in the story, to a miniature throne of gilt and ivory on a dais where she sat, her Duenna and Court Chamberlain standing behind, her friends settled around her and the entertainment began.

There was a mock bullfight danced by the Company, who came down to show the children. The picadors and toreadors rode on hobby horses, richly caparisoned, and brandished long javelins with gay streamers; the matador was one of the Company's leading young men while the bull was a born comedian who charged and made a splendid fight to shouts of 'Bravo, toro ...' When he was killed his head came off to show his laughing face.

There were puppets and jugglers, the gypsies with their gypsy music, some of them the Queen's Chase older boys and girls, among them John and Charles who would carry the monkeys. Mr Adams, their trainer, had brought them, two small brown ones with long arms and sad-looking sagacious eyes. 'Don't shrink away,' he told the boys as he put them on their shoulders. 'They're perfectly tame and friendly. Just be nice and gentle to them but remember, monkeys' paws are cold so don't flinch when they hold on to you.'

The monkeys did not seem to mind; one put its arm round John's neck, the other suddenly began to search through Charles's hair. 'He thinks you've got fleas,' said Pickles laughing. 'If only he would do it in the performance. Now let's try the monkey dance – I suppose you could call it a quartet – but slowly, very slowly,' he said to Jonah who had appeared to play. 'They have to get used to the music and movement.' They also had to be swung, one boy to another and, 'Go with Mr Adams,' he told John and Charles when they had danced. 'He'll show you.'

Mr Adams had also brought a bear that would dance and stand on its head: Pamela, who was good with animals, would lead it but Miss McKenzie was upset. 'Never, never have live animals in a ballet. The audiences will look at them not at your dancers,' but, 'I might as well have been talking to the wind,' she said. 'To think I used to teach him. Now he's teaching me!' and 'Pickles is bewitched by his ballet,' she told Mrs Challoner. 'He seems to have bewitched the management, too. Those tableaux from the Velázquez pictures.'

'Very effective,' said Mrs Challoner.

'Ludicrously expensive.'

The second act, in the mirrored throne room of the palace, was to open with a series of tableaux from the best-known Velázquez paintings, like *Las Meniñas* which Miss Hurley had shown the children. 'There will be the well-known one of Philip IV in brown and silver,' said Pickles. 'I should have liked Desmond in the famous one of Prince Baltasar Carlos on his pony, but ponies that are that barrel shape are impossible to find. Besides it would have to be a stuffed one or it wouldn't keep still.' He had to compromise with Baltasar Carlos in his hunting dress.

'At least it's a hunting dress,' said Desmond, 'and I have a gun and a big dog.'

Mr Adams had plenty of big trained dogs. 'But I'm still sad that I can't include the one painting I really wanted,' Pickles said in the hearing of the children. 'It's a painting of the little prince who was Don Baltasars's little brother, Prince Philip Prospero. As he was only two years old they brought a chair for him to sit on while he was being painted but the tale is that he had to stand because his pet dog – a small spaniel like a Cavalier King Charles – jumped up and took the chair. Velázquez painted them just as they were, the little prince standing and the dog in the chair. The dog stole the painting,' said Pickles, 'but we can't find a reliable King Charles spaniel anywhere.'

'Am I glad,' said Thomas who, as the youngest and smallest of the boys, had been chosen for the little prince.

'I was to have worn a *frock* and have a rattle on a ribbon.'

It was not a rattle but a pomander, spices carried in a jewelled silver ball, and was supposed to ward off disease. It failed with the luckless little prince. 'He died when he was four,' said Thomas. 'I'm far too old to be him.'

'You'll look small enough on that big stage,' said Miss McKenzie.

'Now I won't be there,' said Thomas in satisfaction. 'Mr Pickles can't find my dog.'

'These spaniels are so excitable,' mourned Pickles.

'Sir . . .'

'Mr Adams says he couldn't guarantee . . .'

'Excuse me, sir . . .'

'In any case I believe they're difficult to train.'

'*Excuse* me, sir.'

'Pity. The one in the painting is irresistible.'

'Sir,' and Salvatore stepped out. 'My sister has a little Cavalier King Charles spaniel; he's irresistible and perfectly trained.'

'No,' said Violetta. '*Mai! No, mai!* Never—'

Salvatore had taken Geoffrey Pick and Miss McKenzie to see Prince. 'I have to go home anyway after rehearsal,' said Salvatore.

'You come too, Jean,' Pickles had commanded.

Mr Ruffino was flattered; he ordered Serafina to make

coffee and brought out drinks but Pickles had no eyes for anything but Prince. 'He's not exactly like the painting but he has the same expression. I must have him.'

'No!' said Violetta, 'No! *Mai!* Never.' And Pickles, who always had his own way came up against this six-year-old who, for all her prettiness and violet blue eyes, was firm, stubborn, with a mutinous small face. 'No,' said Violetta. 'No! *È il mio. Mio!* He's mine.'

'Of course he's yours.' Pickles went down on one knee to make his face level with hers. He was at his most winning – when Pickles was winning he was winning indeed and expected to win. 'We're only asking you to lend him. Wouldn't you like your little dog to go to school with Salvatore?'

'No!' It was a shriek in panic.

'Don't you trust Salvatore?'

'No! *Vatienne!* Go away!' shrieked Violetta and the volcano erupted. She screamed, her eyes blazed. 'I hate you.' She hammered Pickles with her small fists, kicked his shins until Mr Ruffino caught her. 'Papa, tell that man to go away. Prince is mine. *È il mio. Mio!* Papa! Papa!'

'*Basta! Basta!*' implored Mr Ruffino and held her tightly. 'Hush, my darling, hush,' and, 'That is enough,' he said to Pickles. 'I am sorry Mr Pick but I cannot allow you to upset my little girl – not for all the ballets in China.' Violetta quietened at once. 'You must find another dog.'

'There isn't another dog,' said Pickles in despair.

'Pickles, he's not that important,' Miss McKenzie intervened.

'Every detail is.'

'We don't even know he would stay.'

That was too much for Violetta. The anger blazed again. 'Of course he'll stay. Lui e molto intelligente. The cleverest dog in the whole world. He *always* stays. He does what Lottie taught him. Lottie still comes to teach him when she comes home on Saturday afternoons. She says, "Stay", and he stays, *e tò allora*, so there!'

'Hi!' cried Salvatore. 'There is one person I believe Violetta would let Prince go with – Charlotte. Wouldn't you, Vivi?'

'*Si* – yes, but I'll come too with Lottie.' She still glared at Pickles. '*Si*.'

'Please,' Mr Ruffino prompted.

'Per piacere,' said Violetta but, 'È il mio. He's mine.'

'Who is this Charlotte?' asked Pickles.

'The girl you wouldn't look at,' said Miss McKenzie.


'Sit.' Prince sat. 'Stay,' and he stayed even when Lottie went to the far end of the room, until she whistled, a low soft whistle, when he came bounding to be petted and praised.

To her surprise, Lottie had been called to rehearsal.

'Not to dance,' explained Miss McKenzie and she said wryly, 'It seems there's a part for Prince in the ballet.'

'For *Prince*? Not for me?' Lottie could not help thinking.

'Salvatore suggested Prince. He is here with Violetta who says you trained him. Violetta will only let him go if he's with you. Mr Pick wants you to come and show what he can do.'

'Sit. Bow.' Prince gravely bowed his head.

'If he did that as a curtain call!' Pickles was ecstatic.

'You wouldn't need any dancers,' said Miss McKenzie. 'It's only one tableau, thank heaven.'

'I'd like him in the court scenes. They had spaniels like this.'

'Well.' Miss McKenzie gave up. 'But it's evident, if you want Prince you will have to have Charlotte Tew as well.'

'She can be a page,' said Pickles. 'The Infanta's own page. She can walk close behind her with Prince on a ribbon.'

The other pages were boys and, 'What about her hair?' asked Miss McKenzie. 'We're not allowed to cut it.'

'She can wear a hat. A hat with a long feather.'

'She'll have to doff it.' The pages all had to learn to doff their hats when they bowed, making a half-circular sweep. Pickles took an eyeful of Lottie as Miss McKenzie showed her how to doff.

'That's a graceful little chick of yours,' he said when Lottie had gone.

'She should be. She comes from Holbein's.'

'Old Anna Holbein?'

'Yes. Anna Holbein. *She* knew a dancer when she saw one.'

'Give her a wig,' said Pickles meaning Lottie not Madame Holbein. The wig was dark, in a fringe like Salvatore's hair, but it was not the wig Lottie wore for *The Birthday of the Infanta*.

'Charlotte. Have you heard?' Priscilla's shocked face frightened Lottie when Priscilla, who had come hot foot to find her, met her outside the wardrobe room door. 'Have you heard?'

'Heard what?'

'The assessment. Irene has failed.'

'I don't believe it.'

On the two assessment days some of what Mrs Challoner called 'the ballet hierarchy' came to Queen's Chase with Ennis Glyn, Miss Baxter from the senior school and some of the governors.

They were there to assess what Mamzelly called the four Ps: progress, promise, performance and personality. Some children faced them with confidence, more were afraid. A few were right to be afraid; assessments over, inevitably some of the parents had to be sent a letter: 'We regret that X would not benefit by further training ...' which meant he or she was not worth it and would have to leave at the end of the term.

'But Irene!' Lottie was stunned. 'How can she leave when she's dancing the little Infanta?'

'Geoffrey Pick chose her', Mrs St Charles had said bewildered, 'out of all the girls.'

'I'm afraid that was for looks, not for her dancing,' said Ennis Glyn gently. 'Irene's dancing has grown more and more lax and she does not respond. That we can't have.'

All the same, it seemed for Geoffrey Pick's sake that Irene would be allowed next term to come to Queen's Chase for rehearsals and dance the Infanta. 'My little girl in the lead at the Theatre Royal,' Mrs St Charles had been telling all her friends with pride.

'She won't forgo that easily,' said Miss McKenzie but soon it emerged that Mr St Charles had put his foot down: he had flown from Australia. 'He says he has had enough, alone out there, his wife and child in England, and as Irene isn't doing any good she's going straight back to Australia.'

Irene was abruptly taken away. 'She didn't even say goodbye.' Priscilla was hurt but Lottie was glad.

'I wouldn't have known how to say goodbye – or anything else – to her.' She still seemed to hear that high young voice ... 'My dears, you should have seen it,' and over the *pointe* shoes with Mamzelly, 'Charlotte thought of it!' Lottie still winced and 'I'm glad I won't have to see Irene ever again,' she vowed, 'I'll never love anyone like that again.' Suddenly she hugged dear, steadfast, ordinary Priscilla.

'Priscilla will never fail,' that was wise Miss Hurley again. 'She'll never make fireworks but she'll be invaluable in the *corps de ballet*,' and, 'Remember,' Miss Hurley had told the girls, 'for one star dancer the Company needs ten good ones in the *corps de ballet*.'

Priscilla was not given to thinking of herself. 'What will Mr Pickles do now?' she said to Lottie. 'Will it be Sybil or Anne-Marie?'

'Hell and damnation,' Geoffrey Pick had said. 'They can't do this to me.'

'It's not they. It's Mr St Charles,' said Miss McKenzie.

'But Irene is an intrinsic part of my ballet.'

'The little Infanta is an intrinsic part of your ballet, not Irene.'

'Then who? Who? I ask you.'

'Use your eyes,' said Miss McKenzie.

'Charlotte, Mr Pick and Miss McKenzie want you in the Salon and take your shoes.'

*

'You mean,' Lottie could hardly say it, 'you mean you want *me* to dance the little Infanta? But I haven't got fair hair.'

'You've heard of a wig,' said Pickles.

'And you'll wear that fabulous dress,' said Miss McKenzie. 'If you dance as I think you will.'

'What – *what* will Auntie say!' Joy was beginning to seep in, then it clouded. 'I'll have to dance with Salvatore. I don't think I can do that,' said Lottie.

'You know the dance,' was all Miss McKenzie said.

Lottie's whole class had learned the pavane but Geoffrey Pick's pavane was as original as everything he did and had become not only the court dance it was supposed to be; the boy had to be chivalrous, yet mocked his Infanta and she, child as she was, flirted with him behind her fan and sometimes, like real children, they played a musical hide and seek. 'Pavane!' said Miss Hurley. 'It's a little fandango!'

The steps could not have been more simple: three walking steps and close, 'with a little rise on to *demi-pointe* as you bring your feet together,' Miss McKenzie instructed. 'It's really only walking, turning, changing hands.'

'You don't need much technique to dance the pavane,' said Mr Pickles, 'but, by God, you need style,' and, as the days went on he saw that was exactly what Lottie had brought to it. 'Madame Holbein gave you that style,' Miss McKenzie told her. 'Pray God you never lose it,' and, 'I told you so,' she said to Pickles.

She had not been as sure about the flirtatiousness. 'Charlotte's such a little innocent.'

'Don't be so stiff,' Pickles besought her. 'Remember you're Spanish as well as royal.' But as Lottie grew into the part, something woke in her: was it a trace of Henrietta's wildness, long suppressed by Auntie, or was it dancing with Salvatore?

'I expect you're sorry about Irene,' he had whispered when they began.

'I expect you are. Now you have to dance with me.'

'I'd far rather dance with you.'

'Liar.'

It was as if they knocked sparks off one another and 'Better,' called Pickles. '*Much* better.'

'Come on, Lottie,' coaxed Salvatore.

'I've told you . . . don't call me Lottie.'

'Well, come on, Charlotte. Don't you remember Christmas?'

'No,' but Lottie began really to dance.

'Splendid,' called Pickles. 'That's it! Yes, toss your head just like that. A little more glint in your eyes when you look at him,' and Pickles and Miss McKenzie said together, 'Bravo! Bravo! Good girl!'

# CHAPTER XIV

It was the Easter holidays but there was a form: 'All pupils who are dancing in *The Birthday of the Infanta* must return to Queen's Chase immediately after Easter, i.e. the Tuesday of Easter week.'

'Oh dear,' said Auntie when she read it. 'There'll hardly be time.'

Lottie was not listening. 'All pupils'. Prince would be coming with Violetta, then could he be called a pupil now? He's in the court scenes as well as in the tableau so I suppose he could, and Lottie laughed.

'Will he stay still?' Mr Pickles was anxious for the tableau. 'He has to stay on the chair and look out from it all of two minutes.'

'The chair's on the left in the picture,' said Lottie who had studied it. 'If I put a biscuit on the cushion and say

"Trust" and go down right and stand in the wings and Thomas stays still Prince'll look across at me waiting until I say, "Paid for".'

'Let's try it.'

Of course they were not on the stage yet, but in the Salon it worked and, 'Brilliant,' said Mr Pickles. 'Thomas, if you move I'll cut your head off.'

'Oh, I can't wait. How I wish we could get on,' grumbled Pickles. 'These blasted holidays!' and now they were to be shortened by five days.

Good, thought Lottie. She could not wait either.

'Lottie, I am talking to you,' and Auntie said, severely for her, 'Things happen in other places besides Queen's Chase, Lottie.'

'I'm sorry, Auntie. What sort of things?'

'Things you haven't dreamed of. Neither had I but I didn't want to obtrude on you in term time.'

For the first time, Lottie looked, really looked, at Auntie and Auntie was different. She was wearing a dress that Lottie, who knew all Auntie's clothes, had not seen before: it was not beige or grey, it was blue, and her hair had been cut, not, as with Mrs Cuthbert, set, but softly blown dry. She seemed less thin and not at all wan, in fact her cheeks were pink as she met Lottie's gaze, nor was she fluttery. 'Something has happened? What?' asked Lottie.

Auntie did not answer directly, instead, 'I can't tell you how pleased I am you are dancing the Infanta, not only for the honour – though, of course, I'm delighted about that too – but because you are dancing with Salvatore. We do so want you to forget all the troubles and make friends.'

'We?' and Lottie remembered something Mrs Cuthbert had said when she, Lottie, was last home: 'You seem very thick with that boy, Salvatore.'

'Salvatore? I can't bear him.'

'Then why is that car up here all the time? I see it over and over again.'

You would, thought Lottie but aloud she had said, 'I expect it's Sam bringing Violetta to see Auntie.'

'Violetta!' Mrs Cuthbert had said and sniffed.

'Yes.' Auntie nodded. 'Mr Ruffino and I', then, as if she had borrowed Mr Ruffino's words, 'have come to have a great regard for one another and I'm happy to tell you, Lottie, we are going to be married.'

'But', Lottie had to sit down as if her legs had given way under her, 'you're too old.'

Auntie was not offended. 'We are getting on, but I am younger than Mr Ruffino – just – and, Lottie, it's never too late to trust – and yes, to love. Nico – he likes me to call him Nico – has had years of misery and worry. His wife was so ill, Lottie. She – she drank.' Auntie's voice sank low. 'It was she who hurt Violetta.'

There were things Mrs Cuthbert had said which, if Auntie had let them, could have troubled her. 'He's only marrying you, Amy, to get a housekeeper and mother for his children.'

'I don't think he is.' Violetta needed her, Auntie knew that was true, all of them did but especially Violetta. 'Isn't it nice to be needed?' she would have said but it was with certainty she could tell Mrs Cuthbert, 'I don't think he is,' and now, 'Look, Lottie.' She held out her left hand: her third finger had a ring. 'A sapphire. Nico says it matches my eyes. He says he fell in love with me on Christmas night. Oh, Lottie, you didn't know what you did when you gave that party.'

'No, I didn't,' but Auntie had not finished yet.

'The miracle is,' she said, 'that this has come in the nick of time, though Nico doesn't know it yet. It hadn't happened when he asked me, thank God, so that not even Edna Cuthbert can say . . . '

'Say what?'

'That I accepted Nico because I had been given what she would call my "walking papers" from Holbein's, after all these years, and couldn't think what would become of us – you and me.' Then, seeing Lottie's puzzled face, Auntie gave her the final shock. 'Lottie, Holbein's is closing.'

\*

'Holbein's closing? But it can't.'

'It has already, practically – Zanny's gone back to Budapest. Emil is caretaking until the builders come. It's going to be pulled down. I've stopped work. I can't believe it but Nico says I shan't work any more.'

'Then we won't be living here any more either?'

'No, indeed, nor in Soho. Nico has bought a house in Pilgrim's Green. Imagine, Lottie, a whole house for us. It has a garden, plenty of bedrooms—'

'Salvatore! I'll have to live with Salvatore,' but Auntie was prattling on. 'Violetta will have a pretty bedroom next to ours. I know I can manage her and take care of her. Serafina's retiring to Italy.'

'Violetta,' and a thought came to Lottie so big it seemed to blot out all the rest: well, in fairy tales there were dogs that could be so small they can fit in your sleeve and so big they can blot out the sky. '*Prince!*' she exclaimed. 'He'll be with us again. I know he's Violetta's dog now but, in a way, he's mine too.'

'And always will be,' said Auntie.

The flat would be gone. Mr Soper, Miss Dorcas and Miss Dora, Sylvie, Victor and the rest of the budgerigars. Mrs Cuthbert – I'm glad about Mrs Cuthbert – but all Lottie's familiar world was crumbling away. 'But Holbein's can't crumble,' argued Lottie. Holbein's was the reason behind their being, hers and Auntie's, and,

'Where's Hilda?' she flashed. 'What has she been doing?'

'She tried and tried but she hasn't the name or the knack,' Auntie had to say. 'She couldn't make it pay. Gregor Gustave pulled out so she hasn't any money.'

'Madame made it pay when she hadn't any money.' Lottie turned her back on Auntie and went to the window.

'Lottie,' Auntie said presently, 'how many times last term have you thought about Madame – or remembered her? Your first term perhaps, but last term?'

Lottie turned and looked at Auntie.

'Truthfully, Lottie.'

'Except when I took Irene to Holbein's and she—' Lottie broke off – she did not want to talk about that. 'And once when Miss McKenzie said Madame had given me my style – not at all,' said Lottie appalled.

'Things have to come and go, Lottie.'

'Madame wasn't a thing,' and, 'Don't, don't,' cried Lottie. She was thinking of the end of the story of the Infanta when, after the dwarf had seen his grotesque ugliness in the mirrors of the throne room, he died of a broken heart. 'Wake him and tell him to dance for me,' said the Infanta and 'Mi bella Princesa – my lovely princess – your funny little dwarf will never dance again,' and the Infanta laughed, cold and heartless.

Cold and heartless! It's quite right I should dance the Infanta, thought Lottie. I'm cold and heartless, and she thought of the icon in her bedroom, the little light that had not been lit all the time she was at Queen's Chase – I should have asked Auntie to see to it – and now it had been as if it were put out for always. Holbein's was closed but Lottie began to tremble. 'I'm not cold and heartless,' all of her cried out. 'I'm not cold and heartless. I'm not.'

Auntie and Mr Ruffino were married at the little Catholic church in Holly Place, Hampstead.

On the bride's side of the church there were not many people but Mrs Challoner was there. 'Would you come?' Auntie had asked her. 'We feel we owe it all to Queen's Chase.'

'I can't wait to meet Mrs Cuthbert,' Mrs Challoner had teased Lottie.

Mrs Cuthbert had nearly not come. 'I will not have that woman at my wedding,' Mr Ruffino had told Auntie.

Mrs Cuthbert had waylaid him in Verbena Road. 'I am *so* glad, dear Mr Ruffino,' she had said, 'that you have taken pity on Amy.'

'Taken pity?' Mr Ruffino looked at her with dislike.

'Yes. What would she have done, she and Lottie?'

Mr Ruffino drew himself up. 'Miss Tew has done *me* the

honour, the very great honour, of consenting to be my wife. Good morning, madam.'

'But she must come,' Auntie had pleaded. 'I know she says things but, Nico, she's good at heart.'

Mr Ruffino gave a snort.

'She will be so hurt.' And there was Mrs Cuthbert, resplendent in a new hat. Miss Dorcas and Miss Dora were dressed in their best and wore identical toque hats of blue feathers. Mr Soper was spruce, shaved, in a dark suit and bow-tie. Zanny was in Budapest but Emil gave Auntie away. The other side of the church was crammed with Ruffino relatives and friends, some English, some Italian; a cousin, Lorenzo, was best man.

Auntie wore her favourite pale blue – dress, coat and hat, even blue shoes with silver buckles. She carried a bouquet of spring flowers Mr Ruffino had sent her. Violetta, beaming with happiness, was bridesmaid in primrose yellow; she had a basket of primroses and small flowers. Salvatore and Lottie had to stand in the aisle behind her, he in a new suit, long-trousered, with a pale yellow tie, Lottie in a pale green dress.

'Now we're brother and sister,' whispered Salvatore.

'We're *not*! Auntie's my aunt, not my mother.'

'Cousins then.'

'Distant cousins.' (Auntie had always said, 'Don't forget, Lottie, we are distant cousins of Lord Wamphrey.')

'Distant cousins,' hissed Lottie. 'The distanter the better.'

They lapsed into giggles. Mrs Cuthbert leaned out of her pew. 'Children! Will you *please* remember you're in church,' and Violetta turned and looked at them shocked.

'You're spoiling the lovely wedding.' It was the beginning of a wail.

'Hush, dear, hush.'

Mrs Cuthbert made matters worse and Lottie knew the wail would grow loud. Quickly she went forward and whispered, 'Come between Salvatore and me and show us how to be quiet.'

Violetta came but in a moment, detached herself. '*I* have to stand in front.'

'People will look at you,' Salvatore warned in a whisper.

'Let them,' said Violetta loudly.

'I hope Salvatore's going to be nice to your auntie,' said Sam.

He had put white ribbons on the car to drive Auntie and Mr Ruffino and see them off on their honeymoon but now he was driving Lottie who had fetched her things from Verbena Road to spend the night with Violetta and Serafina. 'I shall be out,' said Salvatore. Sam would drive them to school next day.

'This is grand for Vivi,' said Sam as they drove. 'She's

a different child with Prince and you, and your auntie is wonderful with her. You see, up to now she's had no one to think about but herself.'

'She adores Salvatore.'

'Yes, but he's hardly ever there, school and that, and Serafina, she encourages her. She was perfect when Vivi was a baby. Now Serafina drives her wild and, bless her good heart, hasn't a notion how to bring up kids. Yes, it's grand for everyone with Violetta – wouldn't wonder if there are no more tantrums – but I hope Salvatore is nice to your auntie.'

'Why shouldn't he be nice?' asked Lottie. 'He always has been to Auntie.'

'She's his stepmother now,' said Sam. 'Salvatore has no time for mothers.'

'Why?'

'Well,' Sam seemed troubled, 'don't know as I ought to tell you. You're only a little girl but you're part of the family now. The first Mrs Ruffino, she used to drink . . .'

'I know. Auntie told me, and she hurt Violetta.'

'Salvatore was there. He saw it. Violetta was a baby then and Serafina put her on a sofa just for a minute. Violetta started to cry. Mrs Ruffino came in and picked her up – she'd had a deal to drink. She tried to hush her but Violetta wouldn't hush. Mrs Ruffino swore at her then suddenly threw her down. I think she meant to throw her on the sofa but, drunk as she was, she missed and Violetta fell on the hard floor and broke her little hip and leg. They never mended properly. Salvatore was only four then but he won't forget.'

Lottie was shocked into silence. Then, 'Poor Violetta!' she said. 'Poor Salvatore!'

'Where are you going?'

It was a Saturday. Lottie, carrying a bunch of red roses, had come out of the gate of their new house 'Mon Repos' – My Rest – as Auntie and Mr Ruffino had named their house. 'Not a very good name for a house when you have to live with Salvatore,' Mrs Challoner had said but to Auntie and Mr Ruffino and, particularly, Lottie, it was perfection: ample, of red brick, its doors and windows were painted glossy white, its garden had holly trees and laburnums, a pergola of roses, a wide lawn and a rockery. The rooms were bright with chintz and new carpets.

Auntie had given Madame's red velvet curtains to Lottie for her bedroom, though they looked opulent for a schoolgirl. 'I'll keep them always,' she had vowed. The icon was there, the lamp lit: Auntie had promised to keep it burning when Lottie was at school.

Salvatore had a boy's room; he would not let Lottie

into it. 'And Prince is here all the time,' marvelled Lottie, 'and comes with Violetta for rehearsals. It's perfect.'

Now, 'I can't take you with me, Vivi,' she had said when Violetta tried to follow her as she invariably did. 'You stay and look after Prince like a good girl.'

Violetta had become surprisingly good, not only good but happy. She went to school now. 'A small school where they understand her,' as Auntie said. Violetta had friends who came to play with her and Prince. There were still scenes, 'But only now and then,' said Auntie. 'We have learned to weather them and she's growing out of them.' Above all, she loved Auntie, Lottie, Salvatore, Mr Ruffino and Sam, who was still with them and who loved her in return. 'You're not taking Prince?' she had asked Lottie at the front.

'Of course not. He must stay with you,' and Violetta had been satisfied, 'Ciao, bello.'

At the gate, 'Where are you going?' asked Salvatore.

'Somewhere,' said Lottie but, though she put them behind her, he had seen the red roses.

'I know where you're going. Can I come with you?' Can I? Not, I will.

'You'd think it silly,' Lottie nearly said but stopped: if there was one person in the world who would not think it silly that person was Salvatore. Also, though she would not admit it, going to Holbein's was like visiting a ghost;

to have Salvatore might be a comfort. Salvatore, a comfort! 'Come if you like,' she said.

'I do like.'

'I don't know why I clean it,' said Emil, 'when the men will be coming tomorrow.' He was alone in the house and theatre, which seemed large and empty. The house was stripped and shuttered, the theatre closed. 'It'll all be pulled down', Lottie told Salvatore, 'to make a block of flats.'

'Holbein's!' said Salvatore. It was his voice, not Lottie's that quivered.

'But I had to clean it,' said Emil. 'She would have wished it.' 'She' was Madame. Emil looked an old man now. 'Tomorrow I go to join Zanny in Budapest.'

There was no easel in the foyer; the little box office was shut. Emil unlocked the auditorium and let them go in alone, only turning on the lights. Salvatore looked at the rows of empty seats, the balcony with its gilt and lights, the orchestra pit with its empty music stands; the piano shut. It was all sealed in silence. He held out his hand to Lottie. 'Let's go up on the stage.'

The backcloths were rolled up, the lights dark; far up above they could see the shapes with skeletons of ladders, coils of rope, the electrician's footboards. Though Emil had swept it, the stage floor was dusty; their footsteps made tracks in it. Lottie, too, felt she had been swept empty then Salvatore said, 'Let's dance the pavane for her. Give me the roses.'

The pavane was, by now, as perfect as they could make it. 'For the present,' Miss McKenzie had told them. 'There's nothing like an audience to teach you.'

There was an audience now. Lottie and Salvatore both felt it; though it was invisible, it was ranged in the seats, in the whole auditorium, in the orchestra as if the piano had been opened, and it was in the dark red roses Salvatore scattered as they danced.

It was the last time any dancers would dance on that stage. They had done their best and, boy and girl, when the pavane ended, made the *grande révérence*, two steps to the right, curtsy and bow, two to the left to do it again. Then they put on their coats and went home.

At the door of Mon Repos they stopped.

'Thank you,' said Lottie and, 'Salvatore ...'

'Yes.'

Lottie swallowed. 'Sam told me about your mother and Violetta.'

The change was instant. 'My mother and Violetta,' whispered Salvatore and Lottie saw jaunty, hard, self-contained Salvatore begin to quiver. He put out a hand ... Lottie took it and held it.

'I won't talk about it, ever,' she said. 'I just wanted you to know I know.'

Silence. Then, 'I think I wanted you to know,' whispered Salvatore. There was a pause then, 'And I'll tell you something I wasn't going to tell you ever. I love you, Lottie.'

Lottie was so taken aback she blushed. His eyes were as kind and steady as Mr Ruffino's. 'I fell in love with you that first day in the hall.'

'You had a funny way of showing it,' said Lottie. 'Besides, children don't fall in love.'

'Oh, don't they? You fell in love with Irene.'

'I suppose I did. I won't ever do it again.'

'You will,' said Salvatore. 'When we're grown up we'll marry and be together always.'

That settled it and he began to whistle. Lottie did not know what else to do and began to whistle too. Her whistle was stronger than his, she had had so much practice whistling to Prince.

# CHAPTER XV

There was just one week to the first night of *The Birthday of the Infanta*.

Mr Ruffino had taken a whole row of seats and, besides his own relations and friends, he had invited Miss Dorcas and Miss Dora and Mr Soper. 'But Mrs Cuthbert I will not have,' he told Auntie.

'Poor Edna,' said Auntie to Lottie, 'now she really will be out of it,' and Lottie felt an unexpected pang of pity. Pity seemed to have woken in her with *The Birthday of the Infanta* and the dwarf as she saw him danced at every rehearsal by Shaun Donaghue who, though he was a brilliant dancer, had never grown to a man's full height.

'He can dance Puck and, often animals,' Miss McKenzie had said. 'Poor boy, he minds terribly.'

He was kind to Lottie, which made worse the only moment she dreaded in the ballet when the Court

Chamberlain told her the dwarf had died and she bent to look at him and laughed. 'I'm sure I'll cry,' she told Pickles.

'It's crucial for the ballet you don't,' said Pickles, 'So you won't.'

Shaun was more practical. 'You just think how much more difficult it is for me to lie still and be dead. And what would happen if I so much as twitch, and you'll be able to laugh.'

Rehearsals had been moved to the Theatre Royal; the first dress rehearsal had been danced in all the panoply of costume – even Prince had a red collar with golden studs. He was groomed every day. 'Isn't he put off by the orchestra and that great stage?' asked Auntie.

'He might have been born on it,' said Lottie. Indeed, it was not Prince who was put off: Lottie had thought she was used to orchestras – there had been one at Holbein's for every Season – but when the impact of the great orchestra of the Theatre Royal first burst on her she would have lost her wits – and her place – if it had not been for Salvatore.

'But, then, I am accustomed,' he said in his lofty way.

'You've only been in *The Dream*,' retorted Lottie, but it was true he seemed accustomed. Perhaps Salvatore was a dancer in another life, thought Lottie and she was grateful, as she was when he warned her, 'Don't look at the lights.'

Miss McKenzie warned of that too. 'Look at the audience. Dance to them as well as to your partner,' and, as a special warning to Lottie, 'Don't look down at Prince.'

All the same, she had to look after him; Prince was now in several of the scenes but chief of all as the pet dog in the chair for the little Prince Philip Prospero tableau.

'Jean, can't we let him take his bow here?' Pickles cajoled.

'If you want to stop the whole show and break the continuity.' Miss McKenzie was more experienced than Pickles in the ways of audiences. 'And now what's this about letting him run round the stage alone in the opening of the garden scene?' asked Miss McKenzie.

Lottie, too, was worried about this garden scene. 'All those trees and flowers!' And she said in agony, 'What happens if he lifts his leg?'

'All the better,' said Pickles.

'Mr Soper's going to wear a dinner jacket,' Auntie had told Lottie. 'Miss Dorcas and Miss Dora have bought evening dresses. Fancy! But, oh dear, I wish Nico was not so set against poor Edna.'

'Mr Pick, could I see you for a moment?'

'What is it, Charlotte? I'm working.' Lottie had dared to say, 'I know you are, but it's business.'

'Business?'

'Urgent business. Mr Pick, you pay Mr Adams for training the monkeys, don't you?' said Lottie. 'And the bear and the big dogs?'

'I do.'

'You haven't paid me for training Prince.'

He looked at her in astonishment. 'Well! You are a little shrew!' His jacket was on the piano and, half amused, he went to it and took out his wallet but Lottie shook her head.

'I don't want money.'

'What do you want?'

'A ticket. Just one ticket for our first night. In the front of the Grand Circle.'

Lottie sent it special delivery to Mrs Cuthbert.

The first thing Mrs Cuthbert saw as she approached the theatre was a poster of a little dog, a spaniel, silken white with great dark eyes and what seemed to be a smile on his face; beside him was, not two-year-old Prince Philip Prospero but the little Infanta. Mrs Cuthbert came close to look. 'Well I never!' said Mrs Cuthbert.

On the day, Lottie had been sick with nervousness. 'All the best dancers are,' Auntie had told her.

'Don't they ever get over it?'

'Never,' said Auntie but when Miss McKenzie brought

the children up from the dressing room far down below in the basement of the theatre, and Lottie heard the orchestra tuning up, it was as if she were being tuned too, to a pitch of excitement and effort, but all the same, 'I must take Prince out,' she said. 'He must go before we begin.' She had not forgotten that Pickles had said, 'All the better,' and did not agree.

'Well, you can't go in the street in that dress, but I'll take him,' offered Mrs Challoner who had come backstage to see them. 'I in all *my* finery.' Mrs Challoner was in full evening dress. 'Royalty is coming,' she explained. 'I'll take him. I and Violetta.'

Violetta was proud and important in her bridesmaid's dress. She was allowed backstage where her duty was to hold Prince in the wings and keep him quiet until Priscilla, as the Infanta's page, took him on. They were both as quiet as mice.

Miss McKenzie let Lottie look at the auditorium through a crack at the side of the curtain but the lights in the orchestra pit were too bright to see more than semidarkness, though far far back were exit signs lit up. There must be hundreds of people out there, all waiting, breathing, alive. Lottie herself felt alive as never before; she was tingling with expectation.

There was the sound of clapping; the conductor had come in and the dancers who were to take part in the entertainment had already gathered on the stage. The overture ended, the orchestra began again with the lilting, titillating music that ran through the ballet. Then a sound, like a *shirrr*, the curtain going up and the whole stage was full of movement with a medley of gypsy melody, the juggler's theme, the bear's dance, the rousing bull-fight music, the jig of the puppets. Then the child guests began to come in, the little nobles attended by their tutors, duennas and courtiers.

Miss McKenzie shook out the stiff folds of Lottie's dress, gave a final tweak to the rose to see it was firm in the long fair wig, so like Irene's hair. Lottie's grown-up ladies-in-waiting ranged themselves behind her; later, in the tableau picture, *Las Meniñas*, one of them would kneel beside her, the other bend over her and Lottie herself would have to stand, holding her head, eyes, hands in a certain position, still as a little waxwork girl, but now she had to pace, pause, pace. Prince's beribboned lead was in her hand; presently she would hand that to Priscilla. Salvatore, in his silks and velvets, his plumed hat, stepped up beside her, taking her other hand and, 'Ready?' said Miss McKenzie. Then, 'Now.'

All that stayed with Lottie of that evening – and every time she danced the Infanta – was not of herself, though she knew she had danced well, it was the Infanta. Perhaps it was from the hours and days of drilling but she seemed to slip into the Infanta's little satin shoes as easily as if she had been born to them. Salvatore, too, seemed perfectly at home yet danced with every nerve and she took more fire from him. When they moved from the pavane, she to her small throne, Salvatore to stand beside her, she was the Infanta still, imperious, sweet and cruel.

The dwarf was brought in his cage, the moment that had driven her to tears and she laughed and clapped with the others; it was with a mocking smile that she gave him the rose. At the end, the ending she had dreaded, as she bent over the poor grotesque still figure – Shaun lay as still as if he were really dead – she paused, shocked for a moment, a telling moment for the audience – 'How well that child acted!' – then remembered, laughed, stood up, tossed her head, laughed again and went into the gay insouciant little solo Pickles had designed for her. 'I wish I had the last solo,' Salvatore had said, which made her dance it better.

As she danced, the mirrored walls of the throne room lifted, showing the garden scene and she danced away into the garden as the curtain came down.

It was Lottie's and Salvatore's evening but it was Prince's too. When he ran alone in the garden scene, in spite of Lottie's care he lifted his leg – 'Well, he'd done that before,' Lottie defended him – and the audience roared with laughter. He stole the scene in the tableau, even from Thomas looking so tiny and solemn in his scarlet and silver dress with a white pinafore – 'A *pinafore!*' he had said in shame – his pomander hanging from his waist with a tiny golden bell to call his attendants. He had stood perfectly still but it was Prince the audience applauded. 'How did they make a dog do that?'

When Lottie and Salvatore took their last curtain call, Pickles between them, Pickles beckoned to Priscilla to bring Prince on and hand his ribboned lead to Lottie. He whispered, 'Tell Prince to make his bow.'

Lottie led him a step forward. 'Sit,' she whispered. Prince sat. 'Bow.' Gravely he bowed his head. The applause was tumultuous.

'I told you so,' said Miss McKenzie.

'Charlotte. Salvatore.'

Backstage, they were surrounded by Ruffino relatives and friends, a proud tearful Auntie, Miss Dorcas and Miss Dora twittering with excitement. They had brought a posy of violets to put among Lottie's bouquets; there was one from Mr Pick and one which touched her, 'From Shaun Donaghue, your dwarf'. 'You keep that card,' Miss McKenzie told her. She, too, was glowing.

Mr Soper had brought a large box of chocolates. Hilda sent a telegram, though there was nothing from Lion. 'He probably forgot,' said Lottie. Auntie sniffed. Pickles had given them 'Expensive presents,' as Auntie said. 'A brooch for Lottie. A gold tiepin for Salvatore.' The management, another bouquet.

'I've never seen anything like it,' said Mrs Cuthbert. 'To think all this for Lottie.'

'Charlotte. Salvatore.' It was Geoffrey Pick. 'Her Royal Highness would like to see you and you are to bring Prince.'

Into the impressed silence came Mrs Cuthbert's voice. 'There! Haven't I always said, Lottie, that little dog would bring good luck?'

And of course, next day and every day after each performance, Lottie and Salvatore were back at Queen's Chase, two children among all the others working at the *barre* or in the centre. 'Head up. Watch that hand ... that foot. Count. Feel the music.'

Lottie though, to her surprise, was interviewed for a newspaper. 'Just one,' Ennis Glyn had allowed.

At the end, the woman journalist asked her, 'Looking back, what do you think was the most valuable thing Madame Anna Holbein taught you?'

The answer was not at all what she expected. 'Something about a nightingale,' said Lottie. 'I don't remember exactly – so much has happened. But I do know,' she gathered certainty, 'none of it would have happened if I hadn't listened.'